D0402834

CATCH & RELEASE

BLYTHE WOOLSTON

CATCH & RELEASE

YOLO COUNTY LIBRARY
226 BUCKEYE STREET
WOODLAND CA 95695

Carolrhoda LAB
MINNEAPOLIS

Text copyright © 2012 by Blythe Woolston

Carolrhoda Lab™ is a trademark of Lerner Publishing
Group, Inc.

All rights reserved. International copyright secured. No
part of this book may be reproduced, stored in a retrieval
system, or transmitted in any form or by any means—
electronic, mechanical, photocopying, recording, or
otherwise—without the prior written permission of Lerner
Publishing Group, Inc., except for the inclusion of brief
quotations in an acknowledged review.

Carolrhoda Lab™
An imprint of Carolrhoda Books
A division of Lerner Publishing Group, Inc.
241 First Avenue North
Minneapolis, MN 55401 U.S.A.

Website address: www.lernerbooks.com

The image in this book is used with the permission of:
Front Cover and Interior Photographs © PM Images/
Photodisc/Getty Images.

Main body text set in Janson Text Lt Std 11/15.
Typeface provided by Linotype AG.

Library of Congress Cataloging-in-Publication Data

Woolston, Blythe.
        Catch & Release / by Blythe Woolston.
            p.   cm.
        Summary: Eighteen-year-old Polly and impulsive,
    seventeen-year-old Odd survive a deadly outbreak
    of flesh-eating bacteria, but resulting wounds have
    destroyed their plans for the future and with little but
    their unlikely friendship and a shared affection for trout
    fishing, they set out on a road trip through the West.
        ISBN: 978–0–7613–7755–9 (trade hard cover : alk.
    paper)
        [1. Disfigured persons—Fiction. 2. Automobile
    travel—Fiction. 3. Fishing—Fiction. 4. Trout—
    Fiction. 5. Communicable diseases—Fiction. 6. West
    (U.S.)—Fiction.] I. Title.
    PZ7.W88713Tro 2012
    [Fic]—dc22   2011009630

Manufactured in the United States of America
1 – BP – 12/31/11

TO EVOLUTION & THE FUTURE POSSIBLE

A BARBLESS HOOK, PERFECT BEND:

Home

I would have recognized the guy even if he hadn't driven up in a truck with Estes Equipment on the door, wearing an Estes Equipment hat and an Estes Equipment shirt with "Buck" embroidered above the pocket. There's a family resemblance, after all. He looks like somebody took my beautiful Odd and dipped him in an extra layer of meat.

I walk out to meet him more than halfway. I don't want him anywhere near the house if I can help it.

"Where's my brother?" says Buck.

"You know what I know. I saw him three days ago in Portland. He might be headed for the coast."

"Look, they're going to be home soon, and they don't need this kind of grief," Buck says while he takes a step

1

too close and drops his hand on my shoulder. He doesn't grab me or anything; he just lets me feel the weight of his thick hand. "That little asshole needs get his skinny ass back here. Maybe you know more than you think you do. Maybe you remembered something that might be . . . useful."

Little Dog Penny comes down off the porch and starts growling and barking. I don't need her help. I push Buck's hand off my shoulder and shrug, "Can't help. Like I told you, you know what I know. That's it."

"Polly?" Mom calls from the porch.

"I got this," I say; then I turn my back on Buck and walk away.

"You let me know if you hear something," says Buck.

I don't say yes. I don't say no. But, at this moment, I'm not inclined to do Buck Estes any favors. His happiness is not my problem.

"What was that about, Polly honey?" asks Mom.

"Odd. He's not back yet. His brother's all worked up," I say. I pick up a glass and open the faucet. I hold my other hand under the water until it runs cold as the river before I steer the glass under the stream and fill it to overflowing. Then I drink it all down. "Some people just have a hard time letting go," I say.

"You want me to fix you some lunch? I could make soup . . ." says Mom.

"I ate before. I'm going to shower, and then I'm going into town," I can see the question forming on my mom's tongue, so I answer it, "I'm going to get the car checked out. Dad said I should do that before I go to Laramie to scope out the school. Got to get that done and apply if I'm going there this fall."

I can see the worries crawling across my mom's face. It's like watching an ant farm. I can't solve this for her. She needs to develop her own coping skills and strategies. She needs to adjust to her new condition—the situation where I can get in a car and drive off to Wyoming.

"It's a long way to drive all by yourself," says Mom.

"People do it," I say.

The envelope is addressed to me, but the letter inside is for Gramma Dot.

Odd must have carried it around in his back pocket until he found an envelope and stamp. The pages are lumpy, creased, smudged, and must have been wet at least once, because they stick together when I try to flatten them out.

Someday soon, I'm going to deliver this letter and the rest. I just can't deliver them yet, not until I know for sure that Odd's grandma is back. Then I have to call around to all the nursing-care facilities to figure out where to take them. It would be easier if I could just hand them to Buck and let him take care of it, but that won't work. Buck's an asshole. If Odd thought he could trust Buck to deliver them, he could have just sent them to Buck. He didn't. He gave them to me.

I pick up the messages I'm supposed to deliver. The edges are fringed with the little ragged circles that get left behind when you rip a page out of a spiral notebook. I hate those raggedy bits. I hate things that are unfinished and half-assed. Odd doesn't. Odd's just fine with broken, lumpy, lopsided things.

I miss him.

That's why I'll read this letter, even though it isn't meant for me.

Someplace in the world that isn't Cape Disappointment,
I don't think.

Dear Gramma Dot,

I'm beside the ocean. It isn't Cape Disappointment
though, because I zigged instead of zagged when I was
leaving Portland. That girl Polly went back, so I'm alone
now and doing my own navigation—and D'Elegance
brought me to this place. If it has a name, I don't know
it. And I'm the only one here.

This ocean is not big the way I thought it would
be. I can't see the curve of the earth, and if there are
whales or sea monsters out there, I can't see them
either. Fog. From here, that's what I see. When I walk,
the fog lets me see some new things in the direction
I'm going, but if I turn back, the things that used to be
there are gone.

Polly will be bringing this letter. Don't worry if you
don't recognize her. You never saw her before. But you
can trust her. I know that for sure.

There is one thing I really need to tell you—I'm
writing it on another page. You read it every day until I
get back, so you always know

I remember you.

LIVING DAMSEL:

Scablands

"You can see fine out of your left eye. Just drive, you pussy."

He's got his foot off and he's resting his stump on the dashboard. I ball up my fist and hit him as hard as I can. I don't know where the punch is going to land, because he's in my blind spot. I don't care if I club him in the nuts or what's left of his leg. Either would hurt. Either would be fine. I've been listening to him bitch and moan about phantom pains for days and miles, but the asshole still won't cut me some slack.

"You hit like a girl," he says.

I clearly didn't hurt him enough. I jerk the gearshift into drive and get my reward: the sound of gravel under the wheels and the loud scrape of car guts on the edge of the pavement as I pull into the right lane.

"Is that like an insult to you? Calling you a pussy? Saying you hit like a girl?" he asks. It isn't an apology. He isn't curious. He's just probing my defenses. I don't answer. I don't need to give him a new way to burrow in, under my skin.

I'm creeping down the blacktop slowly, so slowly, slow as a little old man wearing a hat, and we all know how slow they drive.

Beside me, the passenger seat makes a familiar purring sound and I know he's reclining.

"It's nice to have a little break from driving Miss Crazy," he says. He probably been working on that one for days, but he finally got to the punch line.

The grey-black of the pavement stretches out and away through a whole lot of nothing until it's no wider than a shoelace. The telephone poles get smaller and smaller as they string out toward the horizon.

"Just look at the telephone poles," Odd says. "See how they get bigger when you get closer? You don't need depth perception out here."

Son of a bitch. It's like he reads my mind.

It occurs to me that I can push the gas pedal to the carpet and get all two tons of vintage Cadillac up to deadly speed and crash right into a pole if I want. If I want, I can put us both out of my misery.

If Odd picks up on that thought, he doesn't mention it.

8

A couple things . . .

1) I am not a pussy. I prefer the term Vagina American. I am not a pussy.
2) Murder-suicide never used to be my go-to response. I used to see things differently.

I miss my eye.

Not as much as I did at first, but I still miss it, especially when it comes to situations like this, when distance and closeness matter. I can't play ping-pong. I can't catch a set of keys if you wing them at me. Those are things that Polly-That-Was could do. Not me. I can't depend on the world, but other than that, I'm doing fine. I'm moving my story down the road. Slowly, slowly, like an old man in a hat, I'm moving my story down the road.

I'd rather be home on the couch watching a monstrous shark and monstrous octopus locked in mortal combat. When I say monstrous, I mean really, really big—so big the octopus can slap a fighter jet out of the sky. Fireball! Wreckage plummeting down and disappearing into the waves with a pathetic sizzle. Did I mention the shark is so big it can pull passenger planes out of the sky? Well, it can. And it did. And I don't know how the pathetic humans are ever going to survive.

Seriously, I don't know. That's the question in every monster movie: how will the humans survive? Not *if*. Not "do they deserve it?" Just "how?" When it comes to this particular shark/octopus/human three-way death match, I don't know, because my mom walked in before the stupid movie ended and told me I had company. Then she turned off the television and opened the blinds. And I sat there, blinking in the way-too-bright sunlight, wearing a faded "Walk for the Cure" T-shirt and the U of M flannel boxers Bridger had given me when it was true-love-forever and he was going-to-wait-for-me because two-years-isn't-too-long-to-wait-for-true-love.

"Want to go fishing?" It was Odd Estes.

I hadn't seen Odd since he got out of the hospital, but I'd seen him plenty during those recovery weeks. He was, in fact, my first and only visitor other than my parents. My friends would have come. Bridger would have come. I know for sure he would have come because of true love and all of that. It just wasn't allowed. I was quarantined to minimize the risk of contagion. Even my dad, when he came, stayed on the other side of an observation window.

But the quarantine didn't apply to Odd, because he was Case Three. I was Case Six. Cases One, Two, Four, Five, and Seven weren't being very sociable because they were dead.

It killed a lunch lady, a newborn baby, and three varsity football players.

Football was probably why it killed them, the athletes, I mean. They played hard. I'm sure they were always a little banged up. A scrape, a blister, that's all it takes. Every little break in the skin is a welcome mat as far as MRSA is concerned. No pain: no gain. Play hurt. It's just a scratch. They were athletes, members of a team. And since they were members of a team, they hung out together, which made it handy for the infection. By the time they got sick enough to go to get it checked out, it was too late. It was already systemic. The doctors carved the soft, dead meat off those guys like they were boiled Thanksgiving turkeys. The doctors grabbed surgical saws and filled the air with the smell of hot bone during multiple amputations. The doctors poured the best medicine straight into those proud, blue veins. It didn't help. Three guys just rotted and died.

As far as the infection goes, the lunch lady, the little baby, and I hadn't been in the locker room—so we didn't catch it there. The lunch lady had a lot of little nicks and burns on her hands. Maybe she touched a doorknob or stair rail or a pen in the front office after the bacteria had found its way out into the classrooms and hallways. I could never really ask or get an answer about how it got to the baby. At some level, I just don't want to know. As for me, I scratched a zit on my face after I touched a desk or a light switch or the handle on the drinking fountain. That's how it got me. Never scratch a zit, kids; it only makes it worse. Boy howdy. No fucking kidding.

Oh, I'm way lucky. I didn't have an embarrassing acne flare-up. Nope, lucky me, I got flesh-eating bacteria— MRSA, the next-gen superbug. It ate my eye and part of my cheekbone. It left behind a mess of bumpy pink scars that twists the corner of my mouth up on one side like I'm a half-finished Joker. But I'm so lucky, I live. That infection should have gone straight to my brain. I should have died quick. But I didn't. I'm a miracle of modern medicine, only the medicine doesn't get much credit, I notice. People say I'm lucky, or I'm blessed, and then they turn away.

I'm not the only miracle.

There's Odd too.

If anybody ought to have died it was Odd. Not because he deserved to die, although, knowing him as I do, I feel pretty confident saying that most of the world wouldn't miss him. That's not it. He should have died because he was right in that locker room, snapping towels with those other naked asses. And he had a little raw place on his ankle where his shoe rubbed him wrong. MRSA got in him and started eating him up. Then it stopped. It stopped killing him, and it stopped attacking people altogether.

The outbreak was over.

It left behind a sprinkle of new graves in the community cemetery. In fifty years, a historian could walk through and never notice. They will never guess that this was the year MRSA came to town. With nothing but the dates to go on, the future might chalk it up to a couple of rollovers without seat belts, crib death, and a heart attack. As medical disasters go, it doesn't compare to the bad old days, like the winter when diphtheria killed brothers and sisters so fast they buried them together in one casket like a huddle of puppies.

But there will be evidence if the historian knows where to look.

It's going to be easy to see the tracks of the flesh-eating monster in the win-loss record for the year. And the section of black-bordered pages in the yearbook is a *dead* giveaway.

I'm in the yearbook too—just check the index. There are a lot of page numbers after "Furnas, Polly" because I was a very busy person. I also really liked to have my picture taken.

"Estes, Odd" has even more numbers after his name—what with the rising sports-star thing. I don't know if he likes having his picture taken, but he has one of those camera-loves-it faces.

He is not immediately repulsive.

But he's got problems.

We all have problems.

And, like I didn't have enough already, Odd showed up.

"How do I look? Be honest. My mom's not being honest."

"You sure?"

"I need to know."

He took a second.

"You look like a mummy."

I put my hand up to my face. Of course, the bandages. He doesn't have X-ray vision. He can't see through that wad of gauze and goo.

"Welcome to the twenty-first century, Tut. See you around." I could hear the crutch-slipper shuffle as Odd left my room and moved down the hospital hallway.

Odd stopped by a couple times a day after that, during little breaks from practicing walking up and down the short hall in the quarantine unit.

The visits were always short. He was just taking a breather while he worked to get strong again. They promised he'd get a new, high-tech foot as soon as he was strong enough, and he wanted it. The crutches were just temporary. The robot leg, that was the future.

Nobody promised me a robot eye.

We never mentioned that we were in the hospital, or why, or that we had never been friends outside of the quarantine ward. It should be obvious why we didn't talk about MRSA. As for why we hadn't been friends before, that is simple: I'm a graduating senior, and he was going to be a junior in the fall. Both of us had other, better, options in the friend department. Until we got stranded in quarantine, that is.

After a few dead-end convos full of long, uncomfortable silences, we found out we had one thing in common. We both like to fish. Neither of us is obsessed or anything, but the occasional day on the river or a spring creek—we're down. So we talked about fishing.

The day I got the letter from Bridger explaining that he understood how I needed time and space to heal . . . and so he wanted to do the right thing . . . and so we would kind of take a little break as far as our relationship . . . and so he wouldn't be coming home for the summer because he was going to go to Portland to work for his uncle . . . kind of like an internship. The day I got *that* letter, Odd and I talked about fishing. The day I had the video-consult with the plastic surgeon and learned that it might be possible to do some more reconstruction and scar revision in the future, but not soon, Odd and I talked about fishing. The day I got my provisional diploma in a manila envelope and realized I would never be joining my friends when they moved the tassels on their caps from right to left, Odd was with me. We talked about fishing.

Odd was released from the hospital a few days before me. He wasn't there to hear the smattering of applause from the nurses when the orderly wheeled me out of the quarantine unit. I could have walked—I'd been getting up and pacing the halls for days—but it's hospital policy. So they rolled me down the wide hall and into the elevator and out the doors, past the oversized aquarium full of not-very-healthy-looking rainbow trout to the passenger pick-up zone. The sunshine was very bright. The world looked funny. My mom marched along beside my wheelchair, clutching a red-white-and-blue Mylar balloon in one hand and stack of disposable bedpans in the other. The bedpans were unnecessary. I'd been able to get up and walk to the toilet for weeks. They were also a very bad sign that my mom wasn't ready for any of this.

My happiness is essential to my mom's happiness. There is nothing weird about that. As long as my perfect future was moving along on schedule, we were both fine.

We had always been close. She supported me in all my extra-curriculars. She was my number-one fan who attended every play, every recital, every game (even though I was only there myself to sell pop and crap at the refreshment booth). But during the hospital stay, while I was delirious and tippy-toeing toward death, she morphed into a mom-bot. When I got home, she followed me into the bathroom—just to make sure I'd be OK. She hovered over my shoulder while I spooned up applesauce and chicken-noodle soup, which was always my favorite—when I was five. And I let her, because it was just easier. She quit her job and spent all her time taking care of me. She became my parasitic twin, or I became hers. Same difference.

A couple of days after I got home, I took the mirrored door off the medicine cabinet in my bathroom. What was the point of looking in the mirror while I brushed my teeth? Or after I washed my face? It isn't like I needed it to put on mascara. Just trying that would probably leave me blind in the only eye I have left. So I got a screwdriver and adapted my environment to my new condition, as was suggested by some handouts I received in the hospital.

One of the screws fell in the sink, and I knocked it into the drain because I still don't know how to reach for things, exactly. I was still in the process of developing coping skills and new strategies for my new condition like the rehab handouts said I needed to do. Then, when I was taking the mirror downstairs to stash it in the basement storage closet, I heard my mom in her room.

She was sitting on the edge of the bed with a wad of soggy tissue pressed over her nose, crying. So I sat down beside her, and we hugged each other like two stray kittens drowning in a flood. We were there for I don't know how long; then, when we were both starting to be able to breathe without little sniffling sounds, Mom said, "Do you want to watch *The View* with me, babykid?"

That's how I ended up on the couch with the clicker in my hand. It turns out, unlike playing ping-pong or putting on mascara, a person only needs one eye to watch TV. The TV never blinks or looks away. It accepts a person unconditionally and is generous with its love—all it asks for is a little bit of attention in return. My mom came and sat beside me during *The View*. I laid my head in her lap—good face up—and she stroked my hair. Then, when lady-TV was over, I rested my head on a pillow with my scar side up and watched monster movies. Between ladies and monsters I was learning a lot about myself.

A few months later, Odd Estes showed up in the middle of *Mega Shark vs. Giant Squid* and said, "You want to go fishing?"

I stood up, wearing the flannel underpants of the guy who didn't love me forever and ever after all, and I said, "Yes."

It was not the last of my bad choices.

HOPPERS:

Natural Bridge on the Boulder

I am ready and waiting to go at the butt-crack of dawn.

I have my rod and vest. I checked on the local hatches and fly-pattern advice online last night. I have the right bugs in my flybook—probably. I don't know for sure where we are going. I have a little blue cooler full of peanut-butter sandwiches, snak-paks of applesauce, and three bottles of iced tea. Thanks, Mom.

Mom is very concerned that I not get thirsty while I'm fishing because she doesn't trust me to avoid temptation. Temptation in this case being water, which there is usually plenty of wherever trout are found. Beautiful, sparkly water. Trout are seriously picky about where they will live. They like water that is cold and clear—purer in some ways than anything that ever comes out of a faucet. Considering all that, it might seem completely reasonable to flop down and guzzle right out of a trout stream. Wrong. Unless a person wants to lose weight overnight with raging diarrhea caused by beaver fever. I am not in a position to lose weight. Thanks to MRSA, I weigh exactly as much as when I was twelve, boobless and scrawny.

So once again my mom's anxiety is not *entirely* irrational, just mostly.

I have plenty of time to think about that while I am waiting for Odd.

The sun comes up. All the way up. I drink coffee sitting on the porch step. A lot of coffee. I have time to process the coffee and visit the toilet. When Dad gets up, Mom makes me a second breakfast of pancakes and little pig sausages, which is nice because eating gives me something to do while I'm waiting. The sun swings around the sky. Lunchtime comes, and Mom calls me in to sit at the table so my chicken soup won't spill.

Then I go and crash on the couch for my afternoon monster fix. Something that looks like a rogue houseplant terrorizes a girl in a car. She shoots it a whole bunch of times. I doubt that bullets will have any effect, but at that moment I hear tires crunching gravel in the driveway. I can also hear Mom's half-running footsteps to the front door while I pull myself into an upright position and ready for takeoff. I know Mom was wishing Odd would never show up. I'd heard her and Dad go around about it last night. Mom was against me going. Dad thought I should: "She needs to do *something*!" That was the last word on the matter yesterday, but today, if Odd hadn't shown up, that would have been fine with Mom.

"Well hi, Odd honey," says Mom, managing to remind me, and probably Odd, that we are only children and she is The Mom.

"Missus Furnas!" Odd is smiling and charming and able to grease the gears of etiquette with a pound of cool butter. "I'm sorry I'm late. I couldn't find anybody to take care of Penny." He opens the door of a big silver-blue car and a squirrelly little dog comes rushing out. It bounds right past him and makes beeline for my mom. Once it gets there, it slithers around her legs a bunch of times before it squats to pee practically on her foot. Mom ignores it mightily.

My mom is not a fan of little dogs. She is not a fan of cats. She is not a fan of goldfish. She grew up on a ranch and is of the opinion that animals have a place and that place is not in her house.

"I brought her chow and her bed," says Odd while he drags those things out of the backseat and brings them to the porch.

"Hey Polly, since we are getting such a late start, I thought we'd go ahead and spend a night or two out, you know? So we won't miss the best times to fish. . . . I saw your dad down at the Loaf'n'Jug—goin' to give some baybeeze to some laydeeze," Odd says with a wink meant for the whole TV audience, "And he said that sounded like a plan. Did he call you?"

No, my dad did not call me—or my mom. I can see she doesn't think this is a plan at all—not at all. But it is kind of out of her hands, and she knows it. Odd has managed to offend her three ways in less than five minutes.

1) He showed up.
2) He made a vulgar joke about my dad, the large-animal vet who will spend most of the day artificially inseminating somebody's cows.
3) He went over her head to my dad—like my dad made the decisions.

So, under her perfectly still exterior, Mom is seething. Come to think of it, Odd has offended her four ways.

4) That damn dog.

Odd trails after me as I go downstairs to get my sleeping bag and tent from the rec room closet.

"Shwuuuu, whwuuu, Snow White, I am your father."

Odd is staring at the cardboard cutout of Darth Vader standing by the ping-pong table. Behind the villain is a mural my mom painted for me when I was little: Snow White and her forest animal friends. Come to think of it, it is a little weird for those two to be together. But I don't think about that, not really. Things like that become invisible when a person sees them all the time.

"Shwuuu, shwuuu, shwuuu . . . You don't know the power of the dark side." Then Odd asks, "Why Snow White? Why not Princess Leia? You seem more like a Leia—or Princess Peach."

"I'm just bringing my one-man tent." I say. I'm not going to talk about princesses. The mirror I took out of my bathroom is in the way, and it topples over onto the floor when I push it with my foot. Seven years of bad luck—or is it thirteen? It's neither; the mirror didn't break. The worst luck happens when the mirror doesn't break. When I pick it up and move to the other side of the closet I see my face. Mirror, mirror on the wall, who's the prettiest of them all? Not me, thanks for asking.

"You don't have a one-princess tent?"

I have a moment when I agree with what Mom never said: better to just stay home. But then Darth Vader catches my eye, and I remember what my dad said last night: I need to do *something*. I might as well start with fishing.

"Should I bring a camp stove? Fuel? Cooking gear?"

"Naw. Gotcha covered. We're burning daylight."

Seriously, he can say *that*, to me, after I've been waiting for him for seven freaking hours?

My mom is still standing on the front lawn. Odd's little dog is still running back and forth and back and forth and back and forth. It doesn't pay any attention to Odd. It seems fixated on my mom. My mom is basically refusing to look at it. She's just staring at Odd's boat of a car.

It is a very unsuitable fishing car. It has a third of an inch of clearance. It is freshly washed and scratch-free. It looks like it gets about 12 mpg highway. It is exactly the sort of car that dealers declare has only been driven by old ladies to church. Well, if it gets banged up or gets its guts ripped out, it isn't my problem. I check in my vest pocket for my waterproof box with my phone, I.D., fishing license, and debit card inside. I'm covered in case of disaster—at least as far as taking this dumb car off the blacktop goes. We toss my crap in the backseat. I wave. Mom smiles a pulled-flat smile. Odd's little dog runs back and forth, but it doesn't chase the car down the driveway as we pull out.

I turn my head a little so I can see my mom in the rearview mirror. She's just standing there like a lawn ornament. Beside her, on the porch, I see I forgot to grab the little blue cooler full of peanut butter and iced tea. I'm on my own. I realize this is the first time I've been more than a hundred yards away from Mom since I left the hospital.

Bye, Mom.

The driver calls the tune on the radio. No argument there. Just like there is no argument about who has to open the gate.

There are rules. There is an etiquette. The driver does not open the gate. The other person does—even if the other person is an eighty-six-pound pregnant granny and the gate is one of those half-assed contraptions made out of three strands of barbwire and a couple of unpeeled twisty lodgepoles. It's kind of hilarious: the same guy who makes a double-quick step to open the door of the Loaf'n'Jug for a stranger will sit and wait for his girlfriend to drag a gate open and closed on the way to a fishing spot. At least that's my experience when I was Bridger Morgan's girlfriend. It's just the way of it.

The gate question isn't really in play at the moment because we are enjoying a little wide-open blacktop. It could all be good but, sadly, the driver calls the tune even on the interstate. Odd reaches over and there is about fifteen seconds of serious godly talk . . . static . . . some South-will-rise-again twang . . . static, and he settles on—I wish I brought my MP3 player, what was I thinking?—local sports talk.

"My brother—he's on two hours a day," says Odd.

". . . lost just two games last year, both of them against state champion . . ." says the radio.

"Your brother?"

"This is his show."

". . . . returns a wealth of talent on both sides of the ball . . ." says the radio.

"I thought your brother sold equipment at your dad's . . ."

25

"Tsst. I wanna hear this," says Odd and cranks up the volume. Well that's my cue. It isn't essential that I know about Odd's brother, who I thought sold combines and lawn tractors. I don't really care. I was just pretending to care because pretending to care is what a nice girl does in a conversation. If that's not required, hey! I'm warm. I'm in a car with cushy deluxe seats. I can feel the velvety upholstery on my pretty cheek. I shut my eyes. My eye. The velvet carries a whiff of old happiness, of nickels and vanilla perfume and cigarette crumbs like the inside of an old woman's purse. I go to sleep.

The crunch of gravel under the tires wakes me up.

"Where are we?" I'm confused. It doesn't look like a fishing access.

"Prairie dog town," says Odd.

"You miss the turnoff for the fishing access?"

"Haven't come to it yet."

OK. I'll bite. "Where are we going?"

"Hole below the Natural Bridge on the Boulder."

"Umm . . . why?" It's a long way to drive to go fishing. There are easier places. We must have driven past a bunch of them already.

"Why not? You got a better idea?"

I got nothing.

"Come on Polly, let's see us some doggies," says Odd, and he pivots around and pushes himself out of the driver's seat.

There is a technique to getting out, I see. Odd has been developing coping skills and new strategies for his new condition. I step out too, into the bright light and dust of the prairie dog town. The wind is blowing the grit around. I stand beside the big interpretive sign like they always have at the state parks, which explains prairie dogs are an endangered species. I'm not really interested in what it says, but it cuts the wind.

"These guys were here when Lewis and Clark came through. Well, not these exact guys..." says Odd, "But there were five billion of the little fuckers. There were prairie dog towns that went for miles... miles, Polly, *miles*. A guy could walk all day and never get out of prairie dog town."

"They carry bubonic plague," I say. My dad is a vet, so that's the kind of thing I know about prairie dogs.

"Lewis and Clark caught one. They had all these guys digging and pouring water down the holes. They caught one and kept it with them like a pet. Then they gave it to Thomas Jefferson," says Odd. That's the kind of thing he knows about prairie dogs.

"We could fish here," says Odd, "Tie some grass or granola bar on the hook and—" He mimes air-casting. "Ga-zing!" He's got an imaginary prairie dog on the line. "Get the net, he's a kahuna!"

I turn my back and walk to the car. I don't want to imagine a fat, furry animal jerked into the sky on a hook. I can hear the prairie dogs whistling and chirping. They want to keep each other safe from danger. Each other is all they got in a dangerous world. It probably isn't going to be good enough.

One good reason not to fish the hole below the Natural Bridge: steep cliffs. Another: fast water that disappears underground into a giant natural drain here and comes blasting out—oh, I don't know, somewhere over in the invisible there, maybe. Welcome to certain death dressed up postcard pretty. It is the sort of place a person needs to supervise small children and pets. That's what the interpretive sign says. That list of those who need supervision should probably include amputees and the visually handicapped too, I'm thinking.

I am so very not happy.

I never used to be afraid of heights—not like *afraid*. When I lost my eye I also lost depth perception, and it turns out that the world is scary damn place without it. Now I need to inch along when I'm faced with a sidewalk curb—or a precipitous limestone cliff. Meanwhile, Odd is sort of lurching along ahead of me. My terror is divided equally between the future where I will see him plunge to his death and the future where I plunge to my death. Those seem to be the only two options.

There is a third, it turns out. We both make it to the bottom.

It's a fine, deep pool, but it would be tricky to cast, to let it drift on the current. The force of the cascade stirs up the water, and it's just not that obvious what's going on down there. It looks fancy, but it isn't the fishiest place on the Boulder. I'm inclined to go a little further, at least until I can set myself up to be downstream from my cast. This is it for Odd, though. I don't know if it is bad judgment about the water and what he can accomplish or even worse judgment in leading us down here, where the best path is often underwater and the next best alternative is rock-hopping from boulder to boulder. Rock-hopping is a thing a one-legged fisherman probably shouldn't do.

I am torn between the need to watch out for Odd and the desire to maybe, actually, fish. Polly-That-Was would definitely choose responsibility to others over self-interest. Post-MRSA-monster me says, "Hey, I'm going downstream." Then I add, "Remember, 'This reever can keel you in a thousand vays.'"

Odd gives me a blank look. I guess he's not a fan of movies about giant people-eating snakes. His loss. Worst case, I'll see him when he floats by and I'll tell his parents he died happy, wild, and free. For now, though, I'm just going to ignore him and go fishing.

I drink from plastic cups at home because I missed the stream of water coming from the faucet and hit the back of the sink so hard a regular glass shattered in my hand. I was going to sew a button back on, but I couldn't thread the needle without my mommy's help. Now I'm going to get a nearly invisible nylon line through the eye of a hook.

My fly book is so pretty, so well organized, so full of things that are too tiny—hello, sweet little Flashback Pheasant Tail Nymph—or too fuzzy-headed to give me a fighting chance of getting the line threaded. Grasshoppers have been helicoptering up under my feet since I got out of the car, so a hopper is good, I got to figure. So I pick a Joe's Hopper from the fly book.

I take my good-luck fishing scissors out of my pocket and give myself a nice, clean-cut line to work with. I steady myself and I hold my breath and it actually works. I've got a fly on. I can fish. It's probably more luck than skill, but I'm adding it to my imaginary list of coping skills anyway: able to thread a fly and tie a hook knot.

Trout have good vision and a hard-earned sense of self-preservation. I can't say I've got research to back it up, but I bet most fish of any size have been jerked out of this water a couple of times. Part of growing up a trout, I guess. That sort of experience makes an impression on their raisin-sized brains, so the fish in this river are cagey fish. They are wily fish. They want to eat, but they know it isn't that simple. They know better than to trust the world. They know happiness sometimes has strings attached. They have to be tricked. The first trick is invisibility. All that takes is a nine-foot rod and a careful approach to the water.

The second trick is to bring the dead to life. The fly at the end of the line is not just deadly but dead. I have to make it look like life, I have to make it look like food. I can do that. I'm a practiced liar.

Fishing is all about lies, and not the ones people tell about the monsters that got away. Fishing is about the lies we tell to the fish and the lies they choose to believe.

I stand up and haul out some line. The reel ticks like I'm winding up a clock; the only other sound is the water talking over rocks. There is a moment—there— that likely-looking place where the current brings the food, that is the moment where I want to the hopper to drop. My first cast falls short. Nothing is where or when it appears to be. Even the rocks are a lie. Light bends when it moves through the water, and the result is deceptive. Things are dislocated. So even the river tells lies, I guess. I just have to adapt. I give myself more line, enough to pull its own weight, enough to build some distance and carry me, or at least to carry my bad intentions. Then I reach out again into the world. I put this moment, I put this moment, I put this moment—here— and the fish consents to believe. BAM! ZING! All that time wound up in the reel unwinds. Let's dance, you fishie, let's dance.

In a moment I will have this fish in my wet hand. I will remove the hook. I will lean forward and place it back in the water, and, after a second, it will dart away. I'll feel the water on my own hands, taking away the traces of slime.

That slime and glow of colors on my memory are all that the trout leaves with me. After the release, I will move downstream a little bit more and cast again.

That's the way it's supposed to go, but it doesn't.

It is a little tiny fish, and the hook isn't in its lip. It's through its eye. Through good and hard, since when I set the hook with the smart tug it pulled the barbless wire point right into the bone. Weirdly, the eye with the hook in it looks as bright and marginally intelligent as the other, perfect eye.

It's blushing: it's a little cutthroat. It's beautiful and it would have been more beautiful tomorrow. Stupid damn fish.

I smack it hard on a rock to stop everything that's gone wrong. Then I take out my pocketknife and slit through the tender belly. I push out the guts with my thumb. I don't check to see what he has been eating, because I'm finished with fishing for the day.

The catch-and-release fantasy is over.

"Shit," says Odd. "That all you caught. Better than me. Total shutout." He looks at the tiny fish again, "That's, like, a bite for each of us. I might go cannibal on you."

I realize that Odd wasn't fishing catch-and-release. He wanted to kill fish. He wanted to eat them. I know next to nothing about Odd Estes, but he fishes for meat. Maybe that is all I need to know.

LIVE BAIT:
Chippy Creek

Odd's as busy as a beaver, a whacked-out zombie beaver, dragging chunks of tree around.

We are at a campground a few miles upstream from the falls. The water here looks like excellent fishing. Much easier to navigate than below the falls. Even Odd could have caught something here, but that's all water under the bridge and way downstream. We are here to eat and sleep. As far as I'm concerned, the fishing is over.

"Alrighty then, I'll get this fire going and cook that fish," says Odd. He has accumulated a heap of branches, roots, and bark in a ring of blackened rocks. He doesn't seem to have any system to it. No "start with the kindling" for Odd. It's just a chaotic slash pile.

It's not going to be a tidy, efficient, campstove dinner.

I'm not especially hungry, which is a good thing, because I might be watching Odd try to get a fire started for the foreseeable future. Or at least that would be the case *if* Odd were sane and stupid instead of just stupid. Turns out, he knows what he's up to—in the way that the guys who build fires at keggers know how to get it done. He pulls a coffee can out of the trunk. When Odd cooks, the essential ingredient is gas-soaked sawdust.

Insto-conflagration. The flames roar into life, and sparks fly up looking for a new home. Smokey Bear would not be happy.

Odd is unconcerned. He takes a couple of six-packs out of the trunk and hauls them down to the creek to sink them so they will get cold. I am deeply surprised. Beer in the trunk, and it only shows up now. There were no empties rattling around in the car. It didn't even smell like beer. In fact the car interior was spotless. It is weird, now I think about it. I know guys are car-proud sometimes, but it's not like Odd's dinosaur Cadillac represents the local masculine standard. It isn't fast. It isn't tough. It doesn't even have decent speakers. It's more like the idea of a car some little kid built out of Legos and living room furniture.

Now the beer's in the creek, and Odd brings out a plastic milk crate with a box of cereal, a cast iron skillet, and a can of Crisco in it.

"Gimme the fish."

So I hand the one-eyed trout to Odd. He sticks it in the pan with a gob of Crisco. He takes some time fiddling with it until he gets it set on the least tippy rocks by the fire. The Crisco melts and runs like clear water. The eye of the trout turns milky white and shrivels. This is a terrible way to cook a fish.

The beers come out of the river cold. I'm thirsty and hungrier than I was before I had a couple of bites of trout to whet my appetite. I pour the first one in me like it was a drink of water.

We both walk down to the river's edge for round two.

Odd cups his hand and squats with his weight on his live leg. He shakes his two hands together. "Hopper," he says. Then he tosses it out onto a still place in the river. A rainbow rises, silver and pink, and sips the bug off the top of the water.

I dive for a hopper of my own but miss. It's hard to know where anything is. How big is that rock? Rocks come in all sizes. Did I miss by an inch or six? The hopper flies right into Odd's chest. He reaches down and picks it off. "For the lady," he says.

I can feel the hooked feet of the grasshopper tugging at the skin of my hand when I pick it up. Then I toss it. A widening, nervous ripple grows out from the place where it lands. And then another circle is born when a little trout bangs the surface and the hopper is gone. We keep catching grasshoppers and tossing them into the water. This is the best kind of fishing. At least I think that is the opinion of the fish. By the time we finish the next beer, the sun drops and the shadows rise up until a river of twilight fills up the whole canyon, and it's too dark for grasshopper catching. Odd pulls the rest of the beer out of the water like a stringer of fish. I see there's a grace in his movements. He doesn't bend or rise or turn with ease, but he moves. He is always moving.

"You're doing good, Odd, with the leg, I mean," I say when we settle beside the fire.

"I'm getting there," he says; he clacks his beer can against the metal below his knee. "This ain't gonna change, so I got two choices. I can blow my brains out, or I can get the fuck on with it. You musta tumbled to that, too, Polly."

I don't tell him all I do is sleep, eat, and watch TV. It's kind of a middle option, it seems to me, frozen between dead and doing something.

I don't drink six beers, but I drink five. The fire dies down. The stars come out—and so many mosquitoes even DEET can't keep them from trying to get at my blood. I unzip my tent and crawl in quick before every vampire bug on the planet can follow.

I am wide awake.

I should be able to fall asleep. I've peed three times and I should be able to fall asleep now. But it is one thing to climb into a sleeping bag and it's another to go to sleep. I slept most of the afternoon in the car, so I'm not exactly tired. I think that the bigger issue is a break in routine. I don't sleep that much at night anymore.

I sleep late in the morning—no school, no job—why get out of bed? I do a lot of evasive nap-taking. If I'm asleep or pretending to be asleep, the mommybot tippy-toes around, tucks me in, but doesn't expect me to look at her or say anything.

When everyone else is asleep, I take my laptop to bed. I look really, really awful by the screen light. I know because I've taken pictures of myself with the webcam on my laptop. And then I proved it wasn't just my opinion. I checked with the whole wide world. **Polly Furnas** just watched TV with her friends Kyle and Cartman. June 8 at 1:22 A.M. **Polly Furnas** has zero friends. June 8 at 1:26 A.M. **Polly Furnas** is playing a little ChatSees. June 8 at 3:22 A.M.

"Welcome to ChatSees random video chat. Enable A/V. Press START to begin."

I still don't really know how long anyone will look at me, because I don't let them look at me for more than a moment. I cast myself out into the world. I drift along on the current. Somewhere out there is a raisin-brain who wants something that I almost am. I catch their eye and there is a moment, a moment of connection. Then the lie breaks and I see the recognition or, as happens more often, it's obvious it's just some pervert whacking off. Am I different than the perverts? Not really. I'm after the exact same thing.

On really bad nights I keep wishing that the next face I'll see when I click will be Bridger's. I wonder how long it will take him to recognize me. Part of me knows that he won't pause long enough to see who I am. He won't pause long enough to see who I was. I click and click through hundreds of strangers all around the planet. It is never Bridger.

Sometimes I'm more pissed at Bridger's mom than I am at him. I want to know why she doesn't just make him do the right thing. He should at least call once in a while until we could both pretend that we were losing interest. Seriously, since that letter in the hospital, nada. And his mom—"Call me Mom-B, Polly"— hasn't called either. I used to eat dinner there every Thursday. She taught me how to make Bridger's favorite mac and cheese, full of Asiago and white cheddar, baked in muffin cups so there is more edge of crispy toasted cheese. We used to go shopping together because we trusted each other to tell the honest truth about how we looked when we tried on clothes.

That's over. I can't trust her to tell me how I look because Mom-B doesn't even want to see me. There was a get-well card in the mail right after I got out of the hospital. A get-well card: when you care enough to do the very least. I opened the envelope. I saw a goofy little dog with plastic googly eyes and a bandaid on its nose. Inside it said, "Heal!" because—haha—that's what you say to dogs. "The Morgan Family," that's how it was signed. No "Love," no "Bridger," no "Mom-B," just, "The Morgan Family."

One-big-happy-family, that was The Plan. But one-big-happy-family involved Polly-That-Was. She was going to be part of The Morgan Family, not me. That Polly saw things differently. That Polly didn't pick off one of dog's plastic googly eyes and flick it across the room, but I did.

Come morning, there is nothing to eat but dry cereal, Lucky Charms, that Odd eats by the handful. Last night's little bit of fish and lot of beer isn't what you would call a sustaining meal. We could probably pull more fish out of the river here. It looks plenty fishy. But then there would be the cooking, which I don't want to do and I sure don't want Odd to do. I think we should just head home. Odd agrees. Maybe he is hungry too.

But Odd has a plan for the way back, not that I know about it. He hangs a left past Mcleod on the Boulder road instead of heading straight to the interstate. There is more than one way home. We'll catch the interstate again at Livingston, that's Odd's plan. He's delaying my food and shower, but he's the driver.

Then he snaps on the radio. We are high enough or there is a transmitter station or something, because the reception is great. I only wish there was anything worth receiving. Turns out there is something I enjoy less than Odd's brother on the radio with his forecast of next season's Class-B football ones-to-watch. What's on now is definitely worse. Last time I heard this song, it was good as true. I could be up high on some ridge and half-drunk Bridger would shout my name into the wind and give me everything he had to give. That was how it was to live. But that asshat Bridger won't be shouting my name anymore. So I just grit my teeth and glare out the window at cows and antelope, because that's what's there. The cows swivel around on their stumpy meat-box legs and stare at us while we pass. I can practically read their minds: "Can I eat it? No. Will it hurt me? No. What should I do? Chew."

Antelope are slightly more interesting. They bounce up and down the hillsides like wind-up bunnies. From a distance they are adorable. They can out-Bambi Bambi in the giant eyes and spindly legs departments. That doesn't make them cute. In fact, it makes them a little creepy once you see one up close.

How they look isn't the half of it, though.

Antelope are sex fiends, and speed drives them crazy with desire. It makes sense, since speed is pretty much all they have going for them in survival-of-the-fittest contest. But they are sort of indiscriminate in their fetish. One attempted to rape a field researcher on a dirt bike. Dirt bikes go really fast, so he was asking for it, from an antelope perspective.

But that isn't even the strangest thing about antelope. They are bloody little murderers before they are born.

Antelope start out as part of a litter. Up to eight eggs are fertilized and find a spot in the mom antelope's generous, two-room womb. Ferocious competition between the siblings begins within days—in fact, they start strangling each other while they are only threads of cells. That thins the unborn herd a little, but it doesn't stop there. As the antelope fawns grow, they basically kick, knock, push, jab any remaining brothers or sisters right out the door a long time before they are ready for that adventure. Little pink antelope fetuses drop to the frozen ground under the sagebrush. It's not like they dot the landscape like wads of bubble-gum at a bus stop. They are sort of a rare find. I have never found one myself, but my dad brought one home to show me once. Being a big-animal vet gives him an interesting angle on what children ought to know.

Suddenly, Odd snaps off the radio.

"You got any brothers or sisters, Polly? Don't look like you got any."

"There's just me. I'm my parents' one and only."

"I'm number three. It took them three tries to achieve perfection." He pauses to zap a smile like there is someone to impress with his dazzely-brights. "My sister Thea was beautiful, but she's dead to us. My brother Buck is—not perfect. Why'd your parents stop with you?"

"I don't know, Odd."

But I do know.

My mom told me when we had our first convos about sex. Bam! Sandwiched between tampons and cramps, she segued into in vitro fertilization and how it isn't always easy to have babies. I don't know how common it is to include that type of information in "the talk," but my guess is not very. At least, when I talked to my friends at school they had all heard the deets about tampons, cramps, and how babies are made—but the cells mixed in a lab dish, not so much. My news was interesting, but way less interesting than what girls with brothers had to say about penises with mushroom tops and penises with turtleneck sweaters, which is all a girl person ought to need to know about circumcision.

I think maybe my mom would love it if I had screwed up and had a baby. She could have had another one that way. But she isn't the kind of person who would plan out whatever would make her happy like a bunch of chess moves. She wouldn't let me be a pawn no matter what she had to gain. So I was well informed.

I understood how I came to be.

I wasn't cooked up the good old-fashioned way.

My parents tried. Nothing came of it.

Then the tests started.

It was an escalating war on the lack of baby.

How did my dad feel when my mom got on the plane and flew to California to get a baby?

He never said.

How did my mom look?

My guess is she looked determined.

They had come to some sort of agreement, those two. And I am the result.

There were four. That was too many. Two went away. That meant twins.

Twins are perfect.

It was going to be twins.

It was going to be twins until my brother? sister? stopped growing. Failure to thrive. That's a nice way to say I hogged the best spot. I refused to share. And the other one shriveled up like a balloon with a slow leak. One week there were two heartbeats. And then there was only one. I was a bloody little murderer before I was born.

I am an only child.

STIMULATOR:
Paradise Valley

"D'Elegance needs gas," says Odd when we wind down and out of the hills and get near the interstate. So he turns in the opposite direction from home.

"What kind of mileage does the Elephant get?" I ask. The name fits the ridiculous, lumbering car. Bridger called his truck Buffy.

"*D'Elegance*," says Odd, "D'Elegance." He points at a curlicue of letters on the wooden dash of the car. "D'Elegance gets ten miles to the gallon, and she's worth every drop."

"I'm sorry. I just wanted . . . look, I'll pay for the gas. OK?"

"Sure," says Odd. "I'm hungry," he says, which explains why we pull into the parking lot of a gas-casino-eat-truck plaza. I'm down with it. I was hungry when I crawled out of my sleeping bag, and a couple of pastel marshmallows are a crappy breakfast.

A few minutes later I'm sitting in a booth with my ruined side leaned up against the window. Odd slides out to head for the casino-and-souvenirs side of the place. He needs aspirin, he says. He has a headache from the reflection on the water. It happens. He'd be better off buying some sunglasses. The sun is not that high yet, and it's going to be glaring while we drive back home. Or maybe he's going to wear the pair of glasses I noticed neatly clipped to the passenger's side sun visor. Sure they are huge as Chihuahua eyeballs, and the frames are a swirly pink that probably looks very fancy on an elderly lady with a lavender updo. But who, exactly, is going to notice that Odd is wearing granny sunglasses? Except me, that is. I'm going to notice and I'm going to enjoy it.

I'm lost in imagining Odd in his granny glasses. The waitress comes up and puts a couple of menus on the table and says, "Coffee, honey?"

I forget myself and I look at her to say, "Yeah, thanks, and milk . . ." but, before I get the words out she sees me, all of me, the real me, and she drops the coffee pot. The glass pot doesn't break, but the hot coffee splashes out when it smacks onto the floor. Some of it must have hit her feet because she yelps and squats down.

"I'm sorry," I say to the top of her head. "I'm so sorry."

Then Odd is beside her and he holds her hand while she gets to her feet. She's flustered but working on it.

He looks her straight in the eyes and says, "Thank you, Vonnie." Maybe he didn't look her straight in the eyes every second. He had time to read her nametag while he was checking out her boobs. "Are you OK?"

She pulls a wobbly smile together and says, "Silly me. We'll get that cleaned up." She never takes her eyes off of Odd's face.

When the busboy comes with a mop he looks at me long enough to prove he can, but mostly he just mops up the mess. He's as skinny as his mop handle. The place is buzzing with customers. There is stuff to do.

Vonnie returns with more coffee. "Ready to order?"

"Sure," says Odd, "Biscuits and gravy—for both of us."

"Sure thing," says Vonnie. The coffee cups are full. She moves Odd's closer to him. Mine she leaves where it is. She's forgotten the milk. And I don't like biscuits and gravy, either.

"I figure," says Odd while he fiddles with the side-view mirror, "We're this close to the park, it seems like a waste not to go."

It seems to me that it's always a waste to go to Yellowstone in the summer. It's crowded and there is too much traffic—and the animals with any sense are chilling up and away from the roads and the swarms of tourists. I'd like to consider myself an animal with sense, so I'm inclined to vote no.

"We can go back over the pass," says Odd.

The pass means high country, above the tree line, banks of deep snow that look blue in shadows. That actually sounds good. That is persuasive.

"You think this fine car can make it?"

"D'Elegance will purr right up the Beartooth."

I'm not sure there is any justification for such a ringing endorsement of our wheels. But what's the downside? Worst case, the brakes go out and we plunge, probably not more than a couple hundred vertical feet, from one switchback to the next and die a horrible death. No, worst case is we get a flat and have to change the tire where there isn't any shoulder to pull over to do it—while being eaten by mosquitoes the size of bats and reviled by motorhome drivers. Because the worst, as I've discovered, never actually kills you. It just humiliates you.

"Sure. We can still be home by dinner tomorrow."

"Alrighty then," says Odd, "Yellowstone it is."

I get my phone. There's reception here, so I touch base with my dad, "Im ok today in ynp."

I have thirteen messages. They are all from my mom. The first one says, "You forgot lunch." I delete the rest without reading them. Then I turn the phone off and put it back in the waterproof box.

Odd removes the clown-size pink granny sunglasses from the visor, but he doesn't put them on. "Here," he says, holding them out in my general direction. "It might be better if you wear these—kind of cover up some of that mess you got there. We need to go in and pick up some groceries before we go in the park. How much you got on you?"

"This." I pull my debit card out of my pocket.

"Alrighty then," says Odd, "and how much is that?"

His question catches me off guard. It isn't nice to talk about money, but I answer before I realize I should tell him that's rude. "Thousands. My college tuition money. Every cent I earned at the Kid-O-Korral plus money my parents have been putting in since I was born."

"Alrighty then," says Odd. "Money is no object."

I don't say no to that, because he's right. Money is no object. What do I need tuition money for now? I'm not exactly really graduated. I never took my AP tests. I'm not going to be registering or paying fees in the fall. What difference does it make how that money gets spent? It doesn't make any difference at all.

I don't tell him there isn't more money where that came from. I don't tell him that Mrs. K of the Kid-O-Korral came out to the house to visit after I got home from the hospital. She brought a bunch of lilacs and a big smile and a weepy hug and whole lot of concern. She and my mom talked, mostly. I didn't really have much to say. A lot of the details about my illness are unknown to me. Things happened while I was in a drug-induced coma. Their conversation seemed to have nothing to do with me, so I just tuned it out.

The smell of lilacs filled the room. Lilacs always remind me of Memorial Day and putting flowers on the graves. It's better to use real flowers, the park department reminds the town every year, because the decorations will be removed in one week. All the teddy bears and artificial flowers and plastic flags left on the graves will be gathered up to make mowing easier. Real flowers can be composted and add to the beauty of our local parks. Those other things? They end up in the dump and a bulldozer comes and pushes dirt over them and buries them.

"Polly . . ." Mrs. K was talking to me, directly, "Polly, honey . . ." and she told me that she had made different arrangements while I was in the hospital. I could have my janitorial after-closing hours back, if I wanted, but it would be better . . . some of the parents . . . confuse the children . . . whole town's having a hard time . . . it would just be better if . . . not actually work with the children anymore. And I joined the ranks of the unemployed.

I just left the lilacs on the table. I didn't put them in water. The sooner they got tossed out, the better. It was so nice of her to bring them.

We choose tortilla chips, refried beans, and some nasty American cheese made out of oil that's pretty much indistinguishable from the plastic wrapped around it. It isn't even cheese. It's "cheese product," but it melts easy, so hey, win. We pick up cookies and a twenty-four-pack of high-octane pop full of sugar and caffeine. We pass on the dark red apples; they are shiny on the outside but always disappointing, sad and pulpy inside the skin. A box of graham crackers, a bag of marshmallows, squares of chocolate.

When we pay at the checkout counter, I look at my feet. With the ugly glasses on and my tangled hair as a wall, I'm hidden. When the time comes, I slide my card through the slot and push the right buttons. That's my part to play. Odd is smiling and "Howzit goin'? Think it's gonna be a hot one? Yeah, goin' to the park. Fishing Bridge, maybe the Firehole."

I'm eavesdropping on my own plans, I guess. They are a little different than I thought.

When we get to the car, I take off the pink glasses. There is no one close enough to see the lumpy scars. I kind of forget them, how they look, because I don't look at them. I did look at them, at first. I stared at them in the mirror. The skin looked polished, almost wet, like I had a big patch of bubblegum plastered over my eyehole—or a pronghorn antelope fetus growing on my face. It looked like chewed gum, too: pink, slightly shiny, and mashable.

After my dad showed the fetus to me, I put it in a sandwich bag and added it to the plastic freezer container marked, "Polly's Collecshun KEPP! DON'T THROW AWAY!" Up to that time, my collection was three dead birds (one of them still had both eyes), a bark beetle, and a slightly run-over water snake. Each was in its own sandwich bag, marked with the date and what it was: SNAK, Baby robin, Chikady. Very scientific. Now I added "antalop feetus."

For all I know, that box is still at the bottom of the freezer in the utility room, waiting for me to add something new.

When Mom found the first bag with dead bird and a smudge of peanut butter in it, she went sort of ballistic and came screaming up the stairs, "No, Polly, No! Don't *ever* do this again."

I was hanging out, waiting for dinner with my dad.

"This is wrong, Polly. Just . . . wrong!" She held the little plastic bag at arm's length. I could see what was in it. My bird . . .

She hit the lever on the trashcan with her foot and dropped the bag.

"Mommy! That's my *bird*! My *BIRD*!"

"Never, never touch dead things, Polly. Never," Mom said and started scrubbing her hands with antibacterial dish soap up to the elbows. "It's not nice!"

I felt all crumpled up. How could it be wrong to keep something that interesting? I thought the freezer was a great solution. It would have got smelly if I stuck it in my sock drawer or my Dollie Dreamhouse.

Dad went and opened the trashcan and took the bag out.

"Looks OK. Come on, Dawn. What's the problem? The freezer is already half full of dead animals. What's the difference between a chicken and a . . ." He looked at the bird in the baggie, "chickadee?"

Mom's mouth was a hard, tight little line that said she thought there was a lot of difference.

"What's the harm? We could double bag it or something. And you won't be surprised next time. Come on, honey. It's OK." My dad was using the same voice he uses to settle nervous animals. He's good at his job. It's a very effective voice. "It's OK."

So that night my collection became formal and authorized, in a large plastic freezer container with my name written in Sharpie marker so there wouldn't be any mix-ups or upsets in the future. The only time I ever looked at my collection was when I added something to it. I'd rearrange the bags and look at the frost crystals growing on the feathers and little scaly feet. Then I'd put the lid back on the box, shut the freezer, and know that everything was safe there, perfectly safe, in the cold and the dark.

Somewhere in a lab at the CDC my eye might be in a freezer, carefully labeled, perfectly safe, and seeing nothing.

D'Elegance slows and turns. Both changes are too sudden to qualify as good driving.

"That might be historical," says Odd, pointing at a tiny white church about the size of a drive-up coffee kiosk. I wish it were a coffee kiosk. I could enjoy another double hazelnut latte way more than another Odd history lesson. When we park in front of it, he adds, "Also, I need to meditate on that fence . . ."

"Meditate?" How long is this going to take?

"I'm gonna meditate on how I magically turned coffee into piss—excuse me, Polly—pee.

"There's probably a public bathroom right over there," I say. "Look, they sell gas. That's a better place." Working at the Kid-O-Korral required a certain vigilance on the where-and-when-to-do-potty front. I sort of dropped my guard though, with Odd being taller than me. I thought he'd be potty trained.

"Nope. Look how pretty this place is. It's perfect," Odd says, then opens the door and heads toward a fence post. I guess I should be happy he didn't decide he had to meditate on the little white chapel itself. After he has committed the crime of public urination, he walks around the little church three times. Then he sits down on the porch steps.

I get out of the car. I'm careful to use the "sing-don't-scream" technique, "Time to go . . ."

Instead of doing the right thing, the thing I want him to do, Odd just spreads his arms out like wings and smiles.

I give up and walk over toward him. I may have to use the "gentle touch on the shoulder to get attention" since "sing-don't-scream" didn't work.

He pats the step beside him. I'm supposed to sit. I sit.

He pulls a plastic bag out of his pocket and says, "Now it's time to medicate. Are you feeling any pain, Polly? It's prescription. Alrighty then."

I only smoke a little bit—just enough to be friendly. But it's good and I'm feeling it. I'm in the right frame of mind to go fishing, no doubt. Paradise Valley is world famous for trout. There are trout to be had. I plan my strategy. An orange stimulator would be good here. It doesn't matter what's hatching. A stimulator would work because it doesn't look like anything in particular—just lands on the water and everything about it screams "bug!" But when we get back in the car, we roll past every fishing access that could put us on the water. Every turnout is a promise and then, in the rearview mirror, a disappointment.

"I need a job," says Odd.

"How about fishing guide? We can practice right up here," I say.

"Nope, going to The Park," says Odd. There will be no detours or delays, I guess. "And fishing guide?" He says, "Be serious? Where's the future in that?"

Who says there's a future in anything? Who says there's a future?

"So you want me to write you a reference for the Kid-O-Korral? Little kids need more male role models," I say. An employee like Odd would serve Mrs. K right. He would drive her batshit teaching the little boys to pee on the shrubbery.

"You won't catch me doing that wage-slave shit. Service profession? Profession, my ass. Once a wage slave, always a wage slave. And daycare? Damn! That's like being a wage slave to other wage slaves with a side of extra crap and boogers. You might be up for a lifetime of that, but not me."

He's right, a little. When The Plan was in place, I was going to make money wrangling diaper-poopers at the Kid-O-Korral so I could go to university and become a professional wrangler of slightly older kids. Then, after my career was established and we had a good start money-wise, I was going to produce my own poopy-diaper producer. To keep my baby in diapers and my career on track, I'd go back to work. Meanwhile, some not-metamorphasized-me would take care of it nine hours a day, five days a week. Of course, when Bridger pitched The Plan, he'd put a different spin on it. Poop and diapers weren't even mentioned. It was all happily-ever-after as a diamond-ring commercial.

"You ever worked before?" I ask.

"I worked. Football was my job," Odd says. "Football is the place to start. Some places it's basketball maybe, but football is golden, probably anywhere—except Canada—not that Canada matters—except to beavers."

I assume that we have now entered the zone of conversational drift. It's a medicinal side effect. I clamp a smile on my face and wait for the unfunny jokes about beavers. Supposedly guys think of sex every fifty-two seconds. Wait for it. . . . Wait for it. . . .

"Now football," says Odd. And he catches me being the idiot thinking about sex, or at least thinking about guys thinking about sex, but turns out he's still talking about football. "Football sets a person up. You got your guys. You got your recognition. People hear your name. Football is the first step. But now football is out, so I need a job. A job with the benefits of football, if you know what I mean."

I'm pretty sure I don't. I'm pretty sure the benefits of working at the Kid-O-Korral were nothing like the benefits of football.

Odd turns on the radio.

Does everything on the radio suck? Or is it just that Odd is making the choices? Even the ads are dumb— worse than TV, that's for sure, and that's saying a lot. I miss my friend TV. I miss my couch, and I miss my monsters. I want to be home.

"You can talk to me," says Odd, and he switches off the radio.

I don't feel any overwhelming urge to talk. I'm kind of out of the habit. My friend the TV doesn't expect me to hold up my end of the conversation. TV is the best friend ever.

"You can say anything," says Odd.

"Can I say shut up?"

"You can, but I'm listening. I'm just going to listen as long as you need me to listen. So I hear you saying you want me to shut up. But I don't hear you saying you don't want me to listen . . ."

"So, you heard me say shut up?"

"I'm just listening."

"So talking is listening?"

"Yes. Talking is listening."

"If you won't shut up, could you at least make sense?"

"The only person who needs to make sense to you is you."

"That's dumb."

"Yes. It is dumb. It's OK to be dumb. You can be whatever you need to be."

"Fuck. I don't need to be dumb. I need you to just shut up. Is that possible?"

"It's possible, if you make it possible."

"OK. I'm making it possible. All it takes is you shut your mouth and I shut mine. Deal?"

"That isn't the way it works. Communication is a human need. We *need* to communicate."

"Look, if I needed to communicate, I'd do it. But I don't. Can you just turn the radio back on if you need to listen so much?"

"We all need to listen."

"What is this crap?"

"It's not crap. My mom read it in a book."

"What?"

"My mom got a book a few years ago and it told her that the way to talk to guys was to trap them in the car. It's called car therapy. So I expect it now, the talk."

"Talk? Talk about what?"

"Well, with my mom it was mostly about me controlling my impulses and how my dad is an asshole and how she doesn't want me to be an asshole like him."

"And you want me to tell you what? That you are an asshole? OK. You are an asshole. Are you happy now?"

"This isn't about me. It's about you. You need the emotional release of talking. Talking prevents assholishness."

"And now I'm an asshole?"

"Yeah. Although most of the time people say bitch when they are talking about a girl, but yeah, you're an asshole. "

"I'm an asshole because?"

"We are all assholes."

"*Talking* assholes . . ."

"That's progress," says Odd and he turns the radio on again.

"This guy has something a lot of the young guys don't," says the radio, "He knows where he is at. Now the question is 'Can he make all the pieces stick?'"

What guy? What pieces? If Bridger were in the car, I'd try to pay attention. I'd try to be ready to say something that proved I was listening along with him, that we were together. But Bridger isn't here. We aren't together.

I don't need to make the effort to be nice. I don't need to pretend I care about football.

There aren't any bleachers at this game. There is only the field with the lines drawn out in lime and a trailer with a bank of giant sodium lights making the night stark and bright with shadows. The crowd is three or four deep at the fifty.

I'm mostly just here because it is the place to be. More importantly, it's the place to be with Bridger. I'm pretty indifferent to the game. Sometimes, when someone runs like a rabbit—"He . . . Could . . . Go . . . All . . . The . . . Way . . ."—I pay attention, but mostly it's all "That'll move the chains" kind of crap. The game doesn't matter as much as the way Bridger looks down at me snuggled against his shoulder and tugs me closer.

On the field they crash together, some fast shuffling, then the whistle. Number 36 is down, not down flat-on-the-back down. He's down on his knees like he's waiting for the executioner's ax. People move like ants when you flip over a rock, organized but frantic.

Bridger says, "Don't worry. He's OK."

They are cutting Number 36's jersey off with a ragged, tugging blade. Then they unbuckle the shoulder pads. The steam is rising off his back in a boiling cloud, bright in the yellow lights. The others stand around him, breathing around their mouth guards in little puffs. There is heat and there is cold. Number 36's back is hunched, his head is tucked down, and his arm swings a little with his breathing. Every little tick of the second hand is measured in pain. I can see that; the clench of the body after each ragged breath, that's the tell.

The others stand around him like bison, massive in the front quarters thanks to the shoulder pads, but narrow in the ass for speed. You can see the calculation written in evaporating sweat. A broken collarbone means . . . and what they can do about it is . . . and what they can do without Number 36 is. . . .

What can we do without Number 36?

A person could never tell from this moment, frozen in the yellow light, that he has a sense of humor. He wrote funny things on the whiteboards in empty classrooms and everyone, teachers and students, pretended we didn't know who was making us smile. In this moment, he is just a hurt animal, and that's how I remember him.

But none of it matters now, because that game is totally over and Number 36 is totally dead. His broken bone healed. It healed stronger than before. He got faster and bigger and stronger, but none of that matters. Number 36 became Case One. Broken bones mend stronger, but once the bone saw hits you, it doesn't matter how strong the bone is. There might have been jokes inside that carcass once, but now Number 36 has been lowered into the ground. All the blood and jokes are gone out of him, replaced with embalming fluid and silence.

BEAD HEAD PRINCE:
Firehole River

There's a long line of cars waiting to pay the fee and enter the park. Once we get past that, there's another long line of cars stopped to look at a single bison on the naked, scabby hillside. This is somebody's first bison, I guess, and they don't know that there will be milling herds of them a little further down the road. In a few hours, that person will be sick of bison. Bison will seem less interesting than a brown couch in a dentist's office. Bison will be so close to the car it will be possible to hear the poop plopping on the pavement.

"Look, if we're fishing in the park, we need to stop at the store at Mammoth and buy permits. OK?"

"It's your money, Polly. If it makes you feel better, buy permits."

"And you have to use some of my flies. You understand. This is catch and release only. Those are the rules. Not my rules . . . the rules. OK?"

"Alrighty then, trout torturing for sadistic pleasure only. Check."

The cars finally start moving.

"Feel like boiling? The turnout's in a minute."

I think about it. I used to love visiting Boiling River. Finding the perfect spot between the cold river and the hot springs, complaining about the rotten smell of the clouds of sulfur steam, taking sly looks at shy, almost naked strangers—what's not to love? But now I imagine seeing Odd's robot leg on top of his stack of clothes, like it's normal to remove body parts to go swimming.

"No, it's bound to be too crowded, don't you think?" I say. It's a reasonable answer.

Yellowstone is pretty much living up to my expectations. It's a people zoo. The parking lots at the store are full. We have to drive past to park at the base of the terraces, which isn't that far, except now I worry about Odd walking. I mean, he made it to the bottom of the falls and back up afterward, but he has to be hurting after that effort. I know I am. At least this little walk is fairly short and level, but Odd doesn't head the right direction. He starts up the boardwalk to the thermal features like that was the plan. It was not the plan. I made the plan, and climbing up hundreds of steps in the company of hundreds of people was not part of it.

Water sparkles in the sunlight while it trickles down stone steps. Pretty, pretty, pretty.

A bride in a frothy white dress is having her picture taken with the Opal Terrace in the background. She is a little toy bride standing by sugared shiny tiers of cake. Delicious. Good enough to eat. The breeze shifts and a cloud of sulfur steam surrounds her like a veil. She laughs and buries her nose in the bright bouquet in her hand. Then she grins and sticks out her tongue. She is beyond beautiful. She is adorable. People clap and take pictures. They share her happiness. The world has come to her wedding. They are all her honored guests.

I have three hope chests at home, waiting for when I get married. It's bizarre. It was even bizarre before I was a monster. Nobody does hope chests anymore. People just register for what they want. But I have three hope chests because they are part of my mom's plan for my happy future. One hope chest belonged to my grandmother. It is full of family albums and baby clothes I wore and things that belonged to my grandmother—even her wedding band. She took it off before she died and said it wasn't right to bury a promise. That's the legend: "It isn't right to bury a promise."

The second box holds a kitchen-full of five-ingredient-cook-from-fresh cookbooks and heart-shaped muffin pans. I have a whisk and a ricer and pepper mill. I have an entire set of everyday dishes. I have a stand mixer and an espresso maker. I have lots of things my mother never uses when she cooks, but I have them because my happy future might require that sort of thing.

The third box is the oldest one. My mom looked for the right chest for years before she settled on an antique with hand-sawed dovetail joints and cheerful painted hearts and joined hands and flowers in an emblem on the front. This one is mine, although it probably used to belong to some other pioneer bride who is deader than dust and doesn't need it anymore. It holds bedding mostly. Star quilts made on the reservation, a down comforter from France, pillowcases with hand-tatted lace. Only the best. Because that's what my happy future is all about: only the best.

My mom keeps the keys to the hope chests in her jewelry box. I can get them anytime I want, but she wants to make sure they don't get lost, and I might lose them. What would happen to my happy future then? What?

I see Odd high above me, climbing the stairs to the top of the terrace. He's waving his arms around. It's some sort of performance for a knot of Asian tourists. I doubt they asked for it. I doubt that matters to Odd. I jam my hat on my head and put on the disgusting glasses. My plan is to buy a fishing permit. My plan is good. It's the right thing to do. I turn toward the store and go to do the right thing.

The line to get into the store is so long that Odd catches up with me before I get to the counter to buy our fishing licenses. I ought to feel good that he's going to have a permit, but I just feel irritated that he will spend no time waiting. I did all the waiting. I'm scowling, but it is pretty ineffective. Even if I took off the hat and glasses, the change in expression would be pretty subtle. And then there is the fact that Odd, who ought to get the message, is as sensitive to the rights of others as a rockslide. He's just going where he's going, doing what he's doing, and a scowl isn't going to put the brakes on that.

When we get out of the store, there's a circle of people with cameras hovering like a respectful bubble around a badger waddling across the grass. The badger seems unconcerned. He is used to life in the people zoo.

"You sing, Polly?"

"No."

"Never? Not even in church?"

"Never. Unless you count 'Itsy-Bitsy Spider' or 'Clean-Up Time' or 'Washing Hands Is Fun To Do' at the Kid-O-Korral. Did you know small children respond better to singing than raising your voice? It's a nice thing to know."

"Great. So you're used to an audience. Check. So, now, let's hear you sing."

"Sing what?"

"Whatever you want. But not 'Itsy-Bitsy Spider'—something a little more interesting."

"Couldn't you just turn the radio back on?"

"Do you want to do it karaoke sing-along? OK. That could work."

"No. I meant, why not just listen to the radio? The people singing on the radio are fine, right?" I'm more than happy to lie about my opinion of Odd's musical taste, if it means I don't have to talk—or sing.

"No. I want you to audition for the band," says Odd.

"What band?"

"The band that will be our new job."

He is certifiable. I am also trapped in a motionless car while we wait for some yahoo to get tired of seeing real live bison. OK. He asked for it.

"Come away, human child
To the waters and the wild
With a faery, hand in . . ."

"OK," says Odd, "not so much of that. Do you think you could cover some Chainsaw Percussion? 'Beer! Beer! Beer! Beer!'" Odd's growling scream just might spook the bison and get traffic moving again. Despite that upside, it's not what a person might call singing. He sounds like the soundtrack for a movie about a pissed-off mutant alcoholic bear.

"That's a song?" It's a legitimate question. I'm not just being a bitch.

"Well, Polly, the genre's gotta fit the look, and the look ain't changing." The words drive Odd's point right through the numb scar tissue to the me underneath. It hurts.

"So maybe no vocals for you," he goes on, "You play an instrument?"

"Clarinet in middle school," I say.

"Clarinet. You, me, and everybody else. There will be no band," Odd crumples up that idea like an empty beer can. Conversation over, he clicks on the radio. It's a relief—a horrible, twangfest relief—to listen to some big-hat from Alabama crow about how cool it is to be him. Country music is all about how great it is to be country. It's like a nonstop party—which might be true, I guess, for people who get paid to sing about how great it is to get paid to sing. According to Odd, I'm unlikely to find out how cool that is for myself.

People think being nice is easy, and maybe it is for some people. But for me it took effort. It was *work*. It meant doing a lot of things I didn't want to do. Smiling and asking Mrs. Morehead if she wanted more cookies during the Ladies Day Tea when she was a mean old biddy who pretended being rude was encouragement—that was hard work. And when my second-grade teacher, Mrs. Carver, said my letter *a*'s looked like little, shriveled-up peas, I worked on my penmanship until the pencil put a groove in my finger. People still ask me to address their wedding invitations so they don't have to expose their own sloppy true selves. But I think this whole being nice thing started with Mom.

Now that I've got an actual brain in my head, I know Mom was probably going to love me no matter what. She went to a lot of trouble to get me in the first place, what with the in vitro and the fertility treatments and all the money I cost. And she actually gave birth to me. But there's more. When she was shopping for donor eggs, she went out of her way to match my dad's genotype. It's like she was shopping for one of those just-like-me dolls, only, for whatever reason—because she loves him? because she hates the way she looks?—the "me" she matched was my dad. I am the result: pale eyelashes like a bald-face cow, red hair, pale eyes, pale skin that sunburns during a TV commercial for a Hawaii vacation. My mom went out of her way, as far as medically possible, to design me so she would find me adorable.

None of that matters to a little kid—at least it didn't to the little kid that was me.

All that mattered was that I wanted my mom to love me, and being nice made her happy. It's very hard to tell the difference between a happy parent and a loving parent. So I had good manners and smiled at the people in the grocery store. I said thank you. I said excuse me. I was always happy to help—even if I really wasn't. I was nice.

And then there was Bridger. Bridger loved me because I was nice. I'm not talking about purity-ring, made-up-swear-words–nice. Bridger was fine with sex, for one thing. But he was a nice guy himself. He volunteered, he got good grades, he had plans for the future. And that's the kind of nice I was, too, when I believed it was worth it, because it was all part of The Plan. I was part of the plan, he was part of the plan, and it was a nice plan.

Then something happened that was not so nice.

No matter how hard I try, I'll never, ever be nice enough to be part of the plan now. I'll never, ever be nice enough for Bridger to love me. I used to be a very nice thing, but now I'm ruined. This is my new condition.

We are stopped again, waiting for giant cows to decide to get off the road. If I reach out the window I could touch a bison with short, straight horns. It was a little red calf last year. It survived its first winter when a lot of others didn't. Now it's all grass and sunshine, baby. Life is good. It is jogging along past D'Elegance, and there is nothing graceful about it. Jolt. Jolt. Jolt. Then it turns. For one minute I'm staring right at it. I see the black, wet nostrils. I see the string of clear slobber spinning out of its mouth. I see the eye that was hidden from my sight, the eye that has been gouged out. The place is still bloody. If that bison weren't running, there would be flies all over that raw meat. One way or another, this animal will be dead. One way or another, all of these animals will be dead.

The Firehole River cuts a deep channel. There is no pussy-footing with a gradual bank at this spot. The grassy mud curls over in a slumping lip and then there's nothing but river, pure and urgent as melted glass. The bison tracks all run parallel to the water, because crossing here would be dumb, and the big, boneheaded hairballs know it.

I actually have a little stretch of water to myself, which is never guaranteed here in the people zoo. This is the piece of river nobody else wanted. There is no good place to park near here, so I had to hike for a ways. The water's gone a little warm, which is a matter of degree considering that this river absorbs trickling streams of steaming thermal runoff every day of the year. There are fish in the water at my feet, and they want to stay there. Lips have been ripped. Photos have been taken. A free lunch is greeted with suspicion.

Suspicious fish, warm water, a place that gets whipped into a froth most days when there isn't snow three feet deep: that's the situation, and it makes me happy. My one advantage is the overcast sky full of clouds that blunt the light. The silhouette cast by bright sun behind a fly can ruin the illusion. The key will be setting that drift to exactly match the current, no drag on the line, no telltale twitch. I can give a little flick that mends the line. I can use tippet fine as a unicorn's whisker, just this side of unethical. I'm the girl who knows how to do that.

Assuming I can get my Bead Head Prince on the line, that is. Bead Head Prince nymph, size 12, be steady, I'm your princess. I hold my breath, and it's on and it's knotted. I'm still not taking chances with my crappy vision, though. I add a bright pink water balloon as a strike indicator. If I get a fish on, I'm going to know it fast as the speed of light, way faster than the time it takes a tug to actually reach my fingers.

And so, you, there under the water, let's dance.

I put this moment, I put this moment, I put this moment—here.

The river teaches me to have a smooth and moving surface, and the air teaches me how to breathe when I cast so my arm doesn't get heavy, and that's pretty much all there is to life until twilight starts to shut down the day and I need to walk back along the blacktop's edge to meet up with Odd where D'Elegance is parked beside a picnic table.

"Catch anything?" says Odd when he sees me coming.

"Nope." There are all kinds of lies told about fishing. This is one of them. I caught three fish, each one prettier and bigger than the last. And I set them all free. But Odd doesn't need to hear that.

"Me neither, but I got my picture took with three Japanese girls. We all made peace signs. They were hot."

"Good thing I wasn't with you then, 'cause I would have scared them off."

"I dunno about that. You might not a had the power. They thought I was real photogenic."

"They said that?"

"I think so. It was all in Japanese, but I'm pretty sure that's what they said." Then he reaches around behind him and picks up a box of cereal and shakes it, "Dinner? We got Lucky Charms and Oreos and stuff to make s'mores. . . . And hey, thanks for loaning me those flies. I lost that Bead Head Prince, though. Sorry for that."

I put my hand into the Lucky Charms box and pull out— mostly crumbs. And a yellow-and-orange marshmallow hourglass. This piece of sugar can stop time . . . or speed it up . . . or reverse it. I just don't know how to make it work. And I don't know what I would want it to do, either. What if I reverse time, but nothing changes and I just have to live through everything again? Who would want that? The hourglass makes a little squeak when I crush it between my teeth. I can feel it dissolving on my tongue. Lucky me. I have no milk for my cereal.

I reach for the red aluminum flask and take a deep draw of water. Only, it isn't water; it stings. It stings all the way down and spurs the tears out of my eye.

"Welcome to flavor country, Polly."

All I say is "Water?"

"Didn't take you for a hard-liquor prohibitionist."

I don't say that I like a sloe gin fizz while I play three-handed pinochle with my parents or that Bridger's mom let us have mojitos on the Fourth of July.

"But, if you want water, you got a river. I only brought vodka," says Odd.

"We can't drink the river. What if it isn't clean? We'll get giardia. We're more susceptible to infections. . . ."

"Hey, if we need to pull over 'cause you get the runs, OK. But you aren't going to get that sick, Polly. Death had a shot at you and passed you right up. He took a nibble out of each of us and spit us back out. Until he gets hungry enough to eat leftovers, nothing we do matters. We could drink pure piss and battery acid if we wanted."

I take another sip from the bottle. I am expecting it this time. It isn't so bad. It might be pure piss and battery acid, but I'm ready for it now.

We pass the flask and the cereal box back and forth in silence for a while. Then the cereal box is empty. Odd takes the plastic bag out and scrounges the last bits that have been hiding under there. He hands me a pink marshmallow heart.

Odd lifts the red flask and says, "To Gramma Dot and Meriwether Lewis." Then he passes the bottle to me. I raise it and say, "To Odd's Grandma Dot? And Meriwether Lewis?"

I feel like I need to join in the toast, but I don't know the particulars.

"You know what, Polly? They are going to sell all her shit. They are gonna sell it all. They are going to sell her furniture and books and even her lawnmower."

I'm ready to say how sorry I am . . . and your grandma wouldn't want you to feel sad . . . and maybe they will let you choose something to remember her by . . .

"So they take her on a fuckin' two-week cruise of the fjords of Norway, like she can be homesick for a place she never been, and then they're just going to take her to the new place afterward and hope she's forgot all about her own home."

"What?"

"Gramma Dot, she's got the Alzheimer's. They say she does. Look, can't a person forget they were making a grilled cheese sandwich? Burnt toast don't mean Alzheimer's. Shit happens. I figure you make enough sandwiches, some are going to catch fire. They could cut a person some slack."

"All she did was burn a sandwich?"

"The curtains caught on fire a little bit, no biggie. My mom didn't even like those curtains. Now they're all, 'It's for her own safety,' and 'It's a nice place,' but you know what? That's crap. They just don't want the responsibility."

I don't have anything to say about this. And, considering everything I heard so far, I don't even want ask what Meriwether Lewis has to do with it.

After about ten minutes Odd says, "D'Elegance, that's Gramma Dot's. It was the last car her and Granpa Odd bought before he died. She calls it Granpa's car. Everything on it is original."

When it is finally too dark to see, Odd says, "She thought I was Granpa Odd once. She grabbed my ass. That was weird."

When I wake up to pee, there is a unmistakable wetness, a sticky heat. I hardly need to touch myself with my fingers to know it's happened. I've got my period. Last time I this happened, I had two eyes. It's been months. Why now? Did my body just suddenly remember it wasn't a child? Is this the first time I have blood to spare? Maybe it's just some biochemical reaction to Odd's monkey-house armpits. Whatever. It's a mess. And I've forgotten the number-one rule of the Vagina American: be prepared. I really doubt Odd or Odd's Gramma Dot has stashed a supply of tampons in the Cadillac for this possibility, so I reach down and pull off one of my socks and sacrifice it. Come morning I can replace it with a wad of paper towels. That'll be fun, sitting on a wad of that mess until we hit a pocket of civilization and I can do better.

Suddenly, for the first time I can remember, I'm afraid of bears. I imagine I smell hot and bloody as an elk roast. My tent doesn't feel safe anymore. It just makes me blind. It makes me listen so hard my cheeks start to ache.

I give up, unzip the tent, and crawl out. The stars are bright enough to make me dizzy, but starlight doesn't open up the shadows. I drag out my sleeping bag and head for the Cadillac. I want a barrier a little more substantial than ripstop nylon. D'Elegance will protect me. When I pull the door shut, all the world has to stay outside. She is my protective quarantine. The backseat is too small to feel comfortable, but I fold my legs up and cuddle my cheek against the velvety cushion. My sleeping bag is warm. It's quieter inside the car. I can't hear the constant motion of water and air. All I can hear is the stuff inside my head. I hear the song.

> Come away, human child
> To the water, and the wild
> With a faery, hand in hand
> For the world's more full of weeping
>   than you can understand.

I hear the song, but it's not in my voice. It's in others' voices, the voices I heard when my mom played the CD over and over again while I was in the coma.

> Weaving olden dances,
> Mingling hands and mingling glances.

She found it in my room on my desk and decided it must be special to me. It wasn't. It was just part of a multimedia thesis on Yeats for English. It was all the versions I could find of people singing and reciting the same poem.

> In pools among the rushes
> That scarce could bathe a star.

I know my mom was sitting there, watching me sleep, because her whisper is all tangled up in the song, "It's OK, Babykid. It's OK. Mommy's here. Mommy's here. Mommy's here."

> We seek for slumbering trout
> And whispering in their ears
> Give them unquiet dreams.

CARNAGE ATTRACTOR:
Elkhorn

They don't have what I need at the gas station. They have tampons, but I need pads, with wings. I'm not being picky, it's a matter of life and death according to Mom. If I use a tampon, I'll die from toxic shock. My body is a compromised system. A two-inch wad of cotton and string can kill me. Everything can kill me.

I pay for the gas. I have my sweatshirt tied around my waist to disguise my lumpy crotch. I've replaced the sock with paper towels: Absorbent? Check. Comfortable? So not.

Odd is leaning against the bumper scratching his cheeks. Whiskers itch, I guess. My problem is bigger than his.

"I need to go to real store, Odd. Like a grocery store or drugstore."

"We could use some real food," says Odd.

"That's right, food and stuff," I say.

"Alrighty then," says Odd.

Odd is pushing a shopping cart. I think we could have made do with a little plastic basket, but he's pushing a shopping cart. If I were on my own with a basket, I could just turn away and hide if another customer comes our direction. I could be stealthy and this shopping trip could be over so fast. But I'm with Odd, and he's steering a cart down the narrow aisles making squealing-tire noises when he turns a corner. I wish we could just go our separate ways, but I'm the one who's paying. He picks up a watermelon and starts thumping his knuckles against it. What's he thinking?

"No watermelon, Odd. We can't eat a watermelon in the car. You can have bananas or oranges . . . no juggling the food . . . we could get stuff for sandwiches . . . that's a lot of pop . . . I don't think we need that much . . . you shouldn't eat Lucky Charms every day . . . I need something . . . here, you just wait here . . ." But he doesn't wait. He trails along behind me with the cart right to the feminine hygiene products.

"Alrighty then. That explains the bearanoia," says Odd. He picks up a bale of super-extra-long-overnight-pads-with-wings.

"Put that down," I say.

"It's OK, Polly. I go to the store for my mom all the time," he says and flips it into the cart.

"That's not what I use."

"What *do* you use?"

"Just shut up for a minute and let me find it."

"Hey," Odd yells at a butcher putting packages of steaks out in the meat cooler, "We need some help..." The butcher turns around and comes over. "She needs... What is it you need, Polly?"

"Look, I'm sorry we bothered you. Everything is under control." I toss a box into the cart. It isn't my brand. Tough shit. Will it kill me? Maybe not. But the humiliation is a sure thing.

At the checkout while I'm sliding my card through to pay, Odd says to the cashier and the bag boy, "She gets really cranky when she's on her period..."

I want to tell him he can't have his Lucky Charms, but I've already paid for them. The bag boy is putting them in the sack.

"Why do you have to act like that, Odd?"

"What?" He's feigning clueless.

"Like that, in the store, like a jerk."

"I was trying to be helpful. And friendly. You're not friendly, Polly. You never smile at anybody."

"Ever been to Elkhorn, Polly? Ever visited a ghost town?"

"I've been to Virginia City."

"Pfft. That's Disneyfied. Nobody sells ice cream in a real ghost town. Ever visit a real ghost town? Ghost town cemeteries are the best. You gotta see a real ghost town cemetery. And I'm gonna fix you up."

"Is it far?"

"Naw. It's just on the way," says Odd. He doesn't say on the way to what. I don't ask.

There are fish in Hebgen Lake, but they are safe from us, even the gulpers that will rise for almost anything. We are driving by on our way to a ghost town without ice cream.

". . . suspected pirate mothership near the Seychelles. There have been seven hundred twenty-six incidents of piracy since January 1, a marked increase in activity despite active multinational suppression efforts," says the radio.

"Hey, Polly, we could be pirates! Think about it. Like old-school pirates. We got the qualifications," he says, and then reaches down and knocks on his robot leg. He's got a point. We might have to get a parrot, and I'd have to start wearing my eye-patch, even though it is uncomfortable, since that is part of the uniform. And I'm skinny enough to be a pirate, at least the ones that show up lately on the TV news.

Pirates makes as much sense as rock stars. Maybe more.

"We'd need a boat," says Odd, "But hey! We can just steal one! That's what pirates do, they steal boats."

A truck passes us towing a green drift boat. It's got smiling, up-turned curves—the better to scoop me up and deliver me to the river of happiness. It would be fine to fish from a boat like that. A boat like that could make a person turn pirate.

". . . released by the Russians after seizing a Russian oil tanker are presumed dead. The pirates' small vessel had been stripped of all weaponry and navigational equipment before they were set adrift," says the radio.

"Alrighty then, not pirates," says Odd.

"We could fish anywhere along here," I say.

"We're going to Elkhorn," says Odd.

"Can we fish there?"

"Like you just said, we can fish anywhere," says Odd, and he just keeps driving past the channels of the Madison River. People come from halfway around the world to fish here, but us? We can fish anywhere, so we just blow right by.

I send my dad a message, "Madison now its all good."

I delete thirty-seven messages from my mom.

"So Odd is a family name, huh? I heard you say Grandpa Odd last night. Is it short for something? Because, you know, it's a bit odd," I say.

"Har-dee-fucking-har," says Odd, "Is your name short for Polyester? Polyhedron, maybe?"

"It's just Polly," I'm a little ashamed of myself. Odd's probably been putting up with crap about his name his whole life. It made me cry when the other kids called me Pollywog on the playground, but Odd has to be a lot worse.

"Odd is a real common name in Norway," says Odd.

He doesn't say another thing to me until we stop for gas, then all he does is ask for the toilet key so he can use it while I pay for the fill-up. The key is attached to a long chunk of broom handle with the words "PEE KEY" written on it. I hand it off to him like a baton in a relay race. When we get back onto the interstate, he rolls down his window and reaches down by his feet. He's still got the pee key. He chucks it out the window.

I just shut my eye and shut my mouth. There is no point in asking him why he needs to be such a jerk. He probably didn't even use that pee key. He probably just wants the whole world to start peeing all over stuff like pack rats. I don't say anything. And he doesn't say anything, right back.

When he finally does talk, it comes out of nowhere.

"Gramma Dot, I lived with her when I was little. My mom tried to kill herself back then. She would have done it, too, but she didn't want to make a mess so she was fiddling around getting everything ready. Gramma Dot just dropped by unexpected and tumbled to the situation. They put my mom in treatment, and after that, Gramma Dot, she took care of me. It was better for everybody."

I don't know how to talk back to that. We don't do crazy in my family. Not like that. Odd comes from crazy people. I look at him. There's nothing to see. But now I know his head is full of snakes, all crowded in there and biting each other. It's been going on so long they are immune to poison. Not to pain.

"I'd take care of her, Polly. If they'd let me."

Elkhorn the ghost town is less dead than I expected. There are trucks and four-wheelers parked around. Someone has hung out laundry. A thin track of smoke rises from the stovepipe on another cabin.

"See that?" says Odd, and he points to a grey, weathered building with a balcony staring out over the town. No Juliet is up there waiting for Romeo. No paranoid lawman with a gun has a rifle waiting for the bad guys. It's a ghost town. Romeo and Juliet are both dead. Lawman? Dead. Bad guys? Also dead.

"Right there, in that building, a guy shot another guy at a dance. They had a little disagreement about whether the band should play a polka or a waltz. That's what my Gramma Dot told me. But come on, I want to show you the coolest thing."

Really? There is something cooler than laundry, four-wheelers, and Gramma Dot's tales of getting shot for waltzing?

The coolest thing is the graveyard. We are using Odd's definition of cool, which includes tombstones with little lambs kneeling on the top to make sure we know there are children buried in that dirt. One of the graves has a full-size tree growing right up through the middle of it. Some of them have fences around them. The dates on the ones I can read say 1889 mostly. Must have been an epidemic, or a school burned down, or some other screwed-up tragedy. Been there. Seen that, the latest version.

Odd is going from grave to grave like an optimistic dog that thinks there might still be a useful bone in one of them. Then he stops, unzips his fly and pees all over a grave.

"Odd! Stop that!" I yell, but it's too late. He just shrugs and zips up his pants.

"This would be an interesting place to die," says Odd.

I look around at the dark trees creeping up on the cemetery and the old graves smothered with purple-flowering knapweed. There's not a cloud in the sky, but there is a jet trail. The wind has blown it into fragments that look like chromosomes. The wind will keep blowing and the trace of the jet will be nothing. The people on that plane are hundreds of miles away already, I figure. They are thinking about wherever the fuck they are going—Minneapolis or some military base, who knows? I look at the dirt again. At the graves and the sagebrush. This place isn't that interesting right now, and I'm alive. I can't imagine being dead would make it better. Odd and me, we disagree on the definition of interesting, too.

"We could be ghosts in a ghost town."

Then Odd reaches into the messenger bag he has slung over his shoulder. I imagine he's thirsty or needs to medicate himself, but instead of the aluminum flask or the prescription baggie, he pulls out a gun. The barrel has a dull shine, like a black snake. I can smell the gun oil. The only sound is a squirrel bitching.

"What will it be, Polly? Polka or waltz."

"I can polka." I don't say that I doubt he can.

Odd says nothing. Then he lifts the gun and points. Not at me. Not this time. He points to my left and a little high. KRAAAK!

There isn't even much of an echo.

"Missed," says Odd.

Missed what? I have no fucking idea what might have been worth obliterating. None at all.

Odd's crazy, and he has a gun.

Once a gun is in the game, everything changes.

He walks behind me down the trail, down the hill. I could run, probably, but I can't run faster than a bullet.

I can feel him at my back like a weight, like a mountain lion a deer never sees until it drops and reaches around to choke out the air and ride out the puny struggle. I can hear his steps, the little difference between the true foot and the fake one. I feel the pine needles and little rocks underfoot and I wish he would slip. I'm listening for that moment—the moment when he slides a little and he has to catch himself. That is the moment when I will run.

But we get to the car, and I'm still waiting for that moment. I open the door and get in. I stare straight ahead. I can hear Odd open the door. I hear the locks click shut. My hand is still on the handle, but I don't know if the automatic lock will keep it shut if I try to get out.

"Put your seat belt on," says Odd. Then he turns the key.

We pull off the main road onto a track between the trees. Maybe somebody pulled some logs out of here with a skidder. Maybe somebody used this place for a kegger. Whatever. The Cadillac drags itself along, its elegant belly in the dirt, thumping on rocks or roots.

When Odd lets the car stop, we aren't far off the road, but we are invisible. Not that there is any traffic to see us in the first place.

"Here we go," says Odd, "Perfect."

Perfect for what?

Perfect for crazy.

You build the fire this time, Polly," says Odd. Then he sits down on a deadfall log and takes off his leg. He looks tired. Tired and crazy.

I start scraping off a bare place to build a fire.

"There's no water here, Odd. What if the fire gets away from us?"

"It ain't gonna get away if you pay attention. Just do it right, Polly. The fire won't get away."

I imagine my bones, some of my bones, left behind after the fire. I imagine somebody poking at my falling-apart ribs and finding the melted slug that ripped through my heart. I imagine the back of Odd's skull all blown out from where he put the gun in his mouth. And there in the imaginary ashes is the gun—and the robot leg. And that's all that's left.

"Ass in gear, Polly. We need that fire."

The air around me is still and hot. The sun won't be gone for an hour. I start picking up branches that shattered off the deadfall.

It's just like T-ball. Everyone can play. Even I can play. Odd's head is the ball. The bat? The bat?

These pine branches are great firewood, tinder-dry and brittle, even the big ones. There is no strength left in them. They are that dead. They are no use to me.

The bat . . . is his robot leg. I don't need to hit a homer. Just try, Polly. Just hit the ball and run.

I move as fast as I can. It's not as heavy as I hoped but there's nothing else right now. Grip and swing. It's good enough. It's a good enough hit. I just let go and the robot leg flies off into the bushes. Be careful with the bat Polly, you might hit someone if you just let it go. I did. I did hit someone. That was the plan. Now run, Polly, run, run.

But I trip and fall hard on my stomach in the dirt.

No I didn't trip.

It's Odd. He's got my ankle, my leg; he's crawling up my body.

I hit him hard but not hard enough.

I scratch for something to fight with. Pine needles, dirt . . . nothing, nothing. I twist over so I can fight back. Now he has a hand over my mouth and both of my wrists tight in the other. So I pull my knee up hard. It doesn't put an end to anything, but his hand slips a little and I buck my forehead into his face.

Scrambling knees, hands, on my feet, by the car.

The door is locked. Back door locked. Other side locked. Locked.

Then I hear Odd. He's sitting with his leg and his stump splayed out in front of him toddler-fashion. He has the keys and he's shaking them over his head. He's laughing. It's not an evil laugh. It's just a gut-busting, funniest-thing-in-the-world laugh. He puts his hand up to his nose and wipes at the blood.

"Shit," he says, "Shit. Suck me sideways, Pollywog."

OK. So that happened.

I'm leaning against D'Elegance and I'm breathing ragged, but I can feel the adrenaline dropping . . .

dropping. I rest my head on the car. I just don't have the energy to do anything else.

"So," says Odd, "Let's heat up them beans and eat nachos." He wings the keys at me.

I grope at space and I miss them. "Dumbass!" I yell, after I hear the keys land. Somewhere there, in the pine needles and the dust, are the keys. And until I find them we can't open the trunk and pull out the can of refrieds and the bag of chips.

Until I find the fucking keys, we go hungry.

"You are such a dick."

"Bitch," says Odd, in a cheerful sort of way, and he crawls back onto the log by the fire. "And get my leg out the brush when you got a chance."

"You should probably carry this," Odd says, handing me the gun. "Things can happen to girls. You might need it."

"Need it for what?"

"Bears, rapers, serial killers, drunk squirrels that want to make a nest on your head . . ."

I reach out and take it, not because I'm afraid of bears or serial killers. I take it because Odd shouldn't have it. It's top-heavy in my hand. The weight is in the barrel, not in the plastic grip and clip hiding inside. I pop the clip. I check the chamber. Unloading a gun is a thing my dad thought a girl should be able to do. He taught me to do that before he taught me how to aim.

"It isn't going to be much use if it isn't loaded," says Odd.

That's the point, I think, but I don't say it.

"Maybe when you get home, you and your mom can have a shoot-out. I bet that woman can fire a rifle from the hip."

"What are you talking about?"

"Your mom. She's fierce. And she's still pretty hot. I'd hit that."

"Stop! Shut up! Shutupshutupshutup!"

"I didn't say I was gonna try. Just that, you know . . ."

"I don't know. I don't want to know. People don't talk like that about moms."

"I'm sorry Polly. I just meant nobody should be able to make you do nothing you don't want to. Not even your mom."

"To Gramma Dot and Meriwether Lewis," says Odd.

"To your Grandma Dot and Meriwether Lewis," I say. When I hand the red aluminum flask back to Odd, I ask, "Why only Lewis? Why not Clark too?"

"Because Lewis kept his shit together for the whole trip, and then he blew his brains out. He probably wanted to do it the whole time, but he didn't. Gotta respect that."

It isn't nice to ask, *So how do you feel about your suicidal mom, then?* but I think it. And Odd must know what I'm thinking, because he answers.

"She had the post-parting depression, my mom."

"Post-partum?"

"Yeah, that. Buck says she was going to kill me first because I gave it to her. He says that was the plan."

"That's not the way post-partum depression works, Odd. You know that? Buck got it wrong. He was just a kid when it happened. He was probably scared and confused."

"He mighta been, back then—but not when he said it. He was in high school. He was an adult. I was six. It was right after everybody decided that mom was better and it was time for me to be part of the family again. I was crying because I didn't want to stop living with Gramma Dot. That's when he told me I was only alive on accident."

Odd gives a twitchy shrug and takes another pull off the flask. "To Meriwether Lewis," he says, then he hands the flask to me. I take a drink, but I don't say anything.

I make sure Odd gets drunker than I do, and then, when he lurches off to pee, I pull my wadded up, bloody socks out of the pocket of my shorts. I shove the gun into one sock and the ammunition in another. Then I shake out my sleeping bag and drop the whole mess in there. There might be better hiding places, but it's good for now.

I'm ready for sleep before Odd is done drinking and poking at the fire with a stick. So I get my sleeping bag and go to D'Elegance. "Welcome home," says D'Elegance, "You can make a little nest on the lap of my back seat. You can pet my velvety cushions. Welcome home."

Welcome home.

The thing about home is that it ought to be a place you remember, but I never saw this room before. My mom was busy here while I was making great strides to recovery in the hospital. My mess, my stuff, is all gone. She painted everything she couldn't replace and replaced everything she couldn't paint. I mean everything. The light switch is new.

It's very clean and serene. Pale lemon, pale honeysuckle, pale pale.

All the stuff I had taped to the walls is gone. It was mostly things the kids at Kid-O-Korral gave me. Blue-painted macaroni whale? Gone. Smeary finger-paint pumpkin? Gone. It wasn't like I was attached to that stuff. I just didn't know what to do with it. Throwing it away didn't feel right. Those things were gifts. At least the little kids thought they were gifts. So I taped them up on my walls. And the valentine heart Bridger made me last year out of a Wendy's receipt when he remembered he'd forgotten it was Valentine's Day? "True LOVE forever"? That's gone too.

The mix of makeup and pens and hair ties on my dresser is gone. Actually, my dresser, the one I had since I was eight, is gone. This one is new. The drawers are bigger, but I don't know what's in them. Maybe my clothes, but maybe not. How far did she go cleaning house? Far enough to find the Altoid tin with condoms in it?

She is determined that the MRSA isn't ever going to get me again. Thing is, I've got it. I will always have the MRSA. It is too late for hand sanitizer. It is too late to kill 99.99 percent of germs.

"Mom. It's beautiful. Thank you." We hug. "But I'm tired. Can I just rest for a while?"

"Oh, baby, sure baby. Do you want me to help you change into some PJs?"

"I just want to lie down."

"OK, baby, OK."

I curl up on my new bed and stare at the wall. I stare at the new art that's there to replace the macaroni whale and true love forever.

I guess it's very serene and spa-like, that art. It's a study in soft folds and muted pastels.

Oh, shit, it's my Blankie. Mom found my Blankie— and she framed it.

My Blankie. I learned to call it my "transitory comfort object" in psychology class. I learned that the little guys at the Kid-O-Korral needed to get weaned away from the ragged blankets, the stuffed bears, the things they liked to touch, to suck, to smell. "Your cozy will be safe in the cubby. You're a big girl now." It was a step toward healthy independence. The whole time I was doing that to the little kids, Blankie was in my pillowcase on my bed at home.

And now Blankie is on display in a shadowbox frame, draped carefully to hide the corner I sucked until it was nothing but a raggedy fringe. Poor Blankie, pinned up in there like a big flannel moth. Poor me, if I need some transitory comfort.

In case of emergency, break glass.

Breakfast is graham crackers, marshmallows, and chocolate. S'mores are too much trouble.

"Do you control your impulses, Polly?"

"What? What impulses?"

"Impulses. All of them. Pick an impulse. Do you like, use the three-question technique or something?"

"I don't know what you are talking about."

"The three-question technique. One: if I do or say this, how will it work out for me? Two: if I do or say this how will it work out for others? Three: if I do or say this, will I be following the rules? Those are the questions. They are supposed to lead to better decisions. So I wonder, Polly, is that how you decide what to do?"

"I do what's right, Odd, if that's what you mean. I know the difference between right and wrong, and I do what's right."

"Well, I was just asking, because it seems to me that you make some pretty strange choices in the impulse-control department," says Odd, and he touches the place where I clobbered him with his leg. "Maybe you could use the three-question technique, too. Just sayin'."

"And be more like you? That's great."

"Yeah. It is," says Odd. He is smiling, and the morning light melts all over him like butter.

"We got a choice this morning, Polly. We can go home, or we can go to Portland and tear Bridger a new one. I'm thinking Portland."

"What do you have against Bridger?" I ask.

"Me? Nothing personal. But you're my friend, Polly, and he treated you like shit."

I don't know if I'd call Odd my friend, but Bridger did treat me like shit.

"Portland," I say. Easy as that, I've got a new plan. I'm going to Portland and tear Bridger Morgan a new one, that crap hound.

CHERNOBYL HOPPER:
Berkeley Pit

"If you look to your right at the crest of the mountains you will see Our Lady of the Rockies right up there," says Odd. He sounds like a narrator on the History Channel or a teacher winding up to talk about a personal obsession.

It isn't obvious what I'm supposed to see. The naked rocks gouge out through the trees . . . and there might be something up there. The color is different.

"She's taller than the Statue of Liberty," says Odd.

I've never seen the Statue of Liberty for real. It gives the impression of bigness in pictures, but from here this giant lady looks like a large grain of rice.

"Butte," says Odd, continuing his voice-over, "The Mining City. A mile high and a mile deep and all on the level. The richest hill on earth."

"A mile high and a mile deep—all on the level? What does that even mean?" I don't expect an answer. Little kids do it all the time. They just repeat stuff they think they hear. Odd's just like a little girl in the dress-up corner of the Kid-O-Korral singing into a hairbrush microphone, "There's a pair of flying eyes and a set of bees."

"Almost a mile above sea level, that's your mile high. The copper mines went down almost a mile deep into the mountain. And 'level'—that's a word play. There was levels in the mines, but it's also saying you can trust Butte. What you see is what you get," says Odd.

We are surrounded by abandoned buildings, places for rent, mansions turned into bed-and-breakfasts, and rickety-looking black towers growing into the sky from weedy empty places.

"Why do you know so much about Butte?" I ask.

"Don't we all? Didn't you take Montana History?"

"No, Odd. I took AP History. Butte didn't come up much."

"So you didn't get to go on the field trip?"

"No field trip to Butte."

"Sucks to be you. The field trip was great. Saw the underground speakeasies, the brothels, Evel Knievel's jail cell. We went to Helena too. I met the governor's dog."

"Didn't do that either. Never met the governor's dog. But I'm pretty sure that isn't on the AP test."

"The stuff on the test is boring. The governor's dog is cool. And if you're friends with a guy's dog, you are friends with the guy."

"Is the governor friends with Penny?"

"Who?"

"Your dog, Penny. Is she, like, a political dog."

"Oh. Yeah. Right. The Dog. Penny. She isn't, like, really *my* dog."

"Whose dog is she?"

"I just got her out of the pound the day we left."

"You adopted a dog and then dumped it the same day?"

"Well, it's not like I shaved it and spray-painted it blue and threw it in a Dumpster. It's with your mom. It's fine."

"My mom doesn't even *like* dogs."

"Huh. Everybody likes dogs. She can always take it to the pound."

"She isn't going to take it to the pound because she thinks it is *your* dog."

"Alrighty then. I'll have to get that cleared up when we get back."

Butte. Welcome to Butte. It's not like Butte doesn't make an effort to be good and pretty and sweet. There are flower beds shaped like Celtic knots. If the petunias are getting beat flat at the moment by the wind blowing grit around in the parking lot, that's not Butte's fault. She is totally doing her best. Look, petunias! But we didn't come here to see petunias. We came to see Butte's most remarkable feature, a monstrous, oozing gouge in the dirt. We came here to see the World Famous Berkeley Pit.

Welcome to Berkeley Pit. It's not just an environmental disaster zone; it's a tourist trap.

The gusts of wind in the parking lot are almost stronger than my legs. I am one delicate, ugly flower. I'm glad to duck into the tunnel that leads to the world-famous hole in the ground, but the wind is even stronger inside. The tunnel must focus it like a funnel. The walls are yellow; at least they look yellow in the fluorescent light.

"This would make a great bomb shelter," says Odd.

Odd is wrong, again. And this time he is so obviously wrong I think it's not even worth mentioning. There are no doors on this tunnel, and the nearest water is poison even without radioactive fallout.

Odd spins around and faces me, "Ka-Chakk." He loads an invisible shotgun. "Ka-Bloo!"

I'm used to being an imaginary gunshot victim. It's an occupational hazard. Every day was the Shoot-Out at the Kid-O-Korral. Bananas are guns. Fingers are guns. Naked Barbie dolls bent in the middle so the legs are the barrel: guns. Even guns are guns. But right now the real gun is in the bottom of my sleeping bag in a crusty sock. I'm invincible.

"This would be great place to hide out," says Odd, then he turns and takes the last few steps out into the sunlight at the other end of the tunnel.

It wouldn't be a good place for a standoff for the same reasons it wouldn't be a great bomb shelter. But I've finally figured out my situation. I'm babysitting. Only I won't get paid. And this particular toddler is bigger than average. Babysitting. It is my damn depressing destiny I guess.

We're alone on the platform at the moment. I'm glad about that. I go and stand at the right edge. If anyone else comes, I'll look normal at first. My ruined side will be observed only by snarls of barbed wire and the hillside made of mine waste. There isn't even any grass on that hill. It is deader than the moon.

"This would be a great place to make a movie," says Odd. "Look at that water."

The water in the pit looks purple and dark in this light. The wind has roughed it up so much it doesn't even shine.

"Something would come up out of that water, out of that pit—" Odd continues.

"That water is poisonous acid laced with heavy metals," I say.

"That's why it would be great. You know, monsters like that shit."

He has a point. During my extended study of monster movies, there were plenty where the key was toxic *something*.

"Yeah, but how would anything even get in there?"

"Maybe somebody gets murdered and the body gets thrown in," Odd says

I lean over the rail. "It would be hard to get a body all the way in. They've got chain link and barbed wire. It's not a straight drop. And humans make lame-ass monsters anyway. They are always sort of remembering being human and being all tortured about being monsters. 'I don't *want to* drink blood. I don't *want to* howl at the moon.' Bunch of whiners. Except for zombies. Zombies have no memories as far as I can tell."

"Well, OK, not human." A raven flew past, on cue. "And not a raven," says Odd.

"Why not?"

"Not fierce enough," says Odd. "I mean, they peck out eyes, but . . . meh. An eagle—nope, I got it. Totally got it. An osprey."

"Well, that's fiercer, but how would it end up in the water? The only reason would be if it saw a fish. It isn't going to see a fish. Not in that."

"An osprey," says Odd, "Is *carrying* a fish, a rainbow trout, and it drops it in there."

"So then we have a dead fish in a lake full of acid. I think the story ends with it dissolving."

"No. Like, a thunderstorm comes up."

And it does look like there is a storm coming; dark sky is clotting up behind the mountains to the east.

"Wham! Lightning hits the giant Mary statue up there. And there is a shot where she explodes. Then lightning hits the water in the pit and Zap! The fish is alive, baby. It's alive! Shocked alive! Like Frankenstein, but it's *FrankenTrout*!

"There's already a movie called *Frankenfish*. And what's so scary about a zombie trout? It's kind of stuck down there. It needs to be bigger. But, hey, the electricity could do that too. You see the cells dividing really, really fast, and then, the next shot, the fish is the size of something... something... something huge." I look at Odd. He totally gets it. He appreciates my genius.

"It's Troutzilla! And it jumps up out of the water," says Odd, waving his arm in an arc like a rainbow, "and SPLOOSH!"

"Acid splashes fuckin' everywhere!" I yell.

At that moment a couple of little kids scamper out of the tunnel and onto the platform. They look at me. They scamper back to the door of the tunnel, back to their mom. She lasers a look at me. I'm supposed to know better. I'm not supposed to speak like that in public. She looks away. I'm not supposed to look like that in public, either.

The happy family moves over to the other side of the platform. The mom is teaching her kids how to ignore bad people, bad people like me. I head back to the gritty parking lot. I can hear Odd's slightly limping footsteps behind me in the tunnel.

Odd pulls into a gas station-liquor store. There are plenty of places that will sell you a gallon of milk and a gallon of gas. There are plenty of places where you can fill up the tank and buy beer by the case. It's a little unusual though, a place with gas and shelf after shelf of vodka and tequila. I suppose an argument could be made that it is a very bad idea, but the place seems to be doing OK.

"Hey, Polly, get us some chocolate," says Odd. I'd rather just run the card through the machine. If I buy candy I have to go in. This isn't a freaking candy store, but the gas is pumped. I get my hat and the pink glasses of relatively less horror and go inside.

Odd comes in a couple of seconds later. He's got his pant leg rolled up so his robot leg is exposed. He heads for the bathroom, but on his way he stumbles, falls against a rack full of chips and snacks, and takes it down with him. In the process he knocks bottles down, off the shelf, thunking on the floor. Most of them just roll, but one of them shatters.

"Oh, shit, man, I'm sorry," says Odd, and he's scrambling, crawling, trying to put bottles back on the shelves. In the process, he's makes a bigger mess. His robot leg flails around and crunches bags of chips. He gets the rack upright, but then it tips onto a different shelf and more bottles go down. Every time he sets one bottle up, three fall down.

The guy behind the counter moves fast. My card, receipt, and candy bar are in my hand and the clerk is beside Odd faster than I could be.

"You OK? Look, don't worry about it. I'll get it squared away. You sure you're OK? You didn't get cut?"

"I'm sorry," says Odd again.

"Hey, just as long as you're OK."

"I'll get out of your way," says Odd, and he heads for the door. Somebody comes from the back with a bucket and a broom.

"Thanks," I say, and walk out the door.

Odd is waiting like nothing happened. If he needed to use the bathroom, he forgot about it. I guess he just needed an attention fix.

I send a message to my dad, "All good."

I delete twenty-three messages from my mom.

We're thirty minutes outside of Butte before Odd reaches into the kangaroo pocket on his hoodie and pulls out a pint of whiskey.

"During Prohibition," says Odd in his history-narrator voice, "Butte moonshiners sold their liquor in small bottles like this labeled as furniture polish." Then he drops the voice, "Let's get polished, Polly. Let's get polished."

I reach out and take the bottle from his hand. A car passes. There is a little girl in the backseat. She waves a naked doll at us and sticks out her tongue.

"I think maybe we should wait on the getting polished until later, maybe," I say. What-to-do-what-to-do-what-to-do to distract him? "I'm going on a trip to Albuquerque, and I'm taking my alcohol," I say.

"No. You're going to Bonner and you're taking your booze. Hey! That's it. That's what you should do, Polly. Write a book for kids. You know, 'A is for...'"

"Not alcohol. That's never going to fly. I'll tell you that."

"Well, monsters, Polly! The little boogers would love a book about monsters."

I'm not so sure about the little boogers' parents, but the distraction is working. I put the bottle into the Caddie's glove box and say, "A is for..."

"Aliens!" says Odd. "Aliens are great."

"A is for Aliens
From dark outer space.
They come here to probe you
And laugh in your face."

"That's it! That's it! Do another one," says Odd.
"OK, let me think. It isn't easy to be all rhymey.

"B is for Bugs
Of gigantic size.
Their blood is called ichor.
Their mouthparts have eyes."

"Bug blood is called 'icky'? I'm disappointed. Meh," says Odd.

"Not 'icky,' *ichor*, i-c-h-o-r. Bug blood is called ichor. It's, like, poisonous, oozy stuff that comes out of festering wounds or giant bugs."

"Alrighty then. Ichor. What's C for?"

C is for Cyclops, the one-eyed monster. I'm not ready to tell the truth. I'm not ready for C.

"What's C for?" repeats Odd, "Blowing shit up! Highly explosive! C4!" He thinks this is hilarious.

We drive. I think. I take an easy way out.

"C is for Creatures
There's plenty of those
That live underwater
And have webby toes."

"Again, not your best work. Is D going to be for Dracula?"

"No, Odd, no D for Dracula. No V for Vampire. No W for Wampyre. No W for Werewolf, either. You know how I feel about humany monsters. Just give me a minute, I'll think what D is for."

We cruise by a sign, Deerlodge. D is for Deerlodge, home of Montana State Prison, but that doesn't work. Another sign warns about picking up hitchhikers, the prison again. It's going to be dark in a couple of hours. We can find a place to camp, and I can give the bottle to Odd and he can self-medicate himself to sleep.

"D is for darkness
Where monsters might hide,
But they're out in the daylight,
Hitching a ride."

"I thought you said no humany monsters. Murderous hitchhikers are pretty humany."

"That's not what I was thinking about," I lie, because that *was* where the thought started, but I'm also telling the truth, because the thought is changing, right now, in my head. "I was thinking about this parasite that infects mice and makes them find cats attractive—because the parasite needs to be in a cat to reproduce. So this parasite moves up into the brain of the mouse and screws around with its brain chemistry and makes it love the smell of cats. So it's like a murderous hitchhiker . . ."

"Bullshit," says Odd. "You were talking about homicidal hitchhikers."

"No. The parasite thing is for real. My dad knows about it because he's a vet. My mom knows about it too. It's another reason we don't have a cat. The parasite doesn't just move from the mouse to the cat, it moves from the cats into another host—like humans. That's why pregnant women shouldn't clean cat boxes. It can cause miscarriages and brain damage. Sometimes it doesn't seem like there is anything wrong and the baby grows up just fine until it's an adult. Then the person just goes blind."

"Polly, you have a dark, dark little mind," says Odd, and he reaches for the radio.

That parasite is pretty disturbing. A thing that rides in your brain and steers you right into danger, because that's what it needs. And what you need doesn't matter, not even to you. You just go along with the parasite's plan.

God gets a lot of airtime on the radio. More than I thought. Way more.

"...unless you accept the talking snake and the burning bush! Examine your heart! Look into your heart! Is there doubt there? Doubt is an offense..." says the radio. But Odd's not in the mood for talking snakes. He turns it off in midsentence.

"Maybe we don't need jobs. Maybe we should start a religion. People are godaholics. We could sell god on the radio," says Odd.

"There's already people selling god on the radio."

"That just proves it works. We just have to make sure that we offer new and improved product."

"Like what?"

"Well, it doesn't have to be totally new. Just different. My Norwegian ancestors had a one-eyed god. What you got?"

"My ancestors believed in magical talking trout."

"Well, there it is," says Odd. "The god is a one-eyed trout."

"But what's in it for the customer? What did that one-eyed god thingy do?"

"All the usual god stuff: made shit up, lived in the sky, stole things, wandered around. How about the trout?"

"It mostly inspired poetry."

"Crap. One-eyed god did that too. What's with the poetry thing? I think we need to leave that part out. Who is going to worship that? Seriously. There is no money in poetry. The one-eyed trout doesn't give a shit about poetry."

"Does it live in the sky?"

"Well, duh! Ever see a rainbow?"

"This could actually work. I mean, a rainbow is pretty convincing."

"But it is also a cutthroat, because of the sacrifice. There's always sacrifice. And it's a golden too. That's why they need to send us the money. "

"And if they don't?"

"That sacrifice thing goes both ways. It's an eye for an eye. In a game like that you don't want to piss off the one-eyed god."

"It would be a mighty, mighty god," I say, "And the name of that god . . ."

". . . Troutzilla!" We say it together because we both know it.

A car passes. It has a Jesus-fish sticker on the back. "Look," says Odd. "We already have converts."

We are off the interstate and driving up the Blackfoot. It's rising twilight by the time we come to a campground and pull off the road. When I open the door, I can hear the sound of the river. There's a cinder-block toilet a little way beyond some trees. There is a picnic table and a fire pit with a grill.

The door on the toilet is heavy and the little room behind it is full of flies. A sign on the wall says, "NO TRASH in the TOILET! PLEASE!!! KEEP lid CLOSED!" The lid is wide open. Nobody plays by the rules. When I'm done, I use the toe of my shoe to close the lid. Not that it matters. The flies don't even notice.

Odd is sitting on the table with the bottle he swiped in Butte in his hand. The plastic milk crate is beside him. The chocolate is gone. The chips and salsa and beans and cheese—all gone. The only thing in the Lucky Charms box is Odd's prescription. We have half a roll of Nekko wafers we found in the glove box, a mushy banana, and a can of Crisco. I'm not sure there's any reason to get a fire started in the grill pit. The best plan may just be to drink myself to sleep. Odd seems to have worked that out already. The vodka flask and the pint of whiskey are on the table, too. It's going to be a three-course meal—four if we eat some Nekkos.

"Why'd you swipe this, Odd?" I ask when he hands me the flask.

"No reason. Just wung it," he says.

"You just wanted it?"

"Naw. I wung it. Wing, wang, wung it. I just wung it."

I open the Crisco and scoop some up with a gray Nekko. Licorice grease. It's what's for dinner.

I check my phone. No bars here. The canyon is steep and there's nothing to do about it. These things happen.

"You know, I think we should still make that movie," says Odd. "And we should both be in it—you know—the way that old fat guy was always in his own movies. The one about those fuckin' birds is the creepiest thing I've ever seen, because that could *happen*. That would be a shitty way to die, pecked to death by birds. And Stephen King, he does that too. So we should totally do that." He takes a few steps away from the picnic table and then lies down on the dirt.

"Want me to pitch your tent for you? It'd just take a minute," I say.

He's still talking about the movie. "You can be horribly disfigured by the acid. I can be a guy who got bit by

Troutzilla and loses a leg. So we're like after revenge and shit."

"Odd, that sounds like *Moby Dick*."

"*Moby Dick*," Odd snorts, "*Moby Dick*. What's bigger than Winnie's poo? Moby's dick. His dick!"

I don't say goodnight. I pitch my tent. I crawl into my sleeping bag. I poke around with my toes until I can feel the lumps. This little bloody sock is full of bullets, and this little bloody sock is full of gun, and this little bloody sock says, "Pee, pee, pee, you can't make me go home." Goodnight socks. Goodnight gun. Goodnight flies. Goodnight scum. Goodnight monsters. Goodnight bears. Goodnight noises everywhere.

"Blemish," says Mom. She points at her own cheek, but I know she means on mine. The damn zit has been bugging me since this afternoon. "Make sure you put something on it before you go to bed—don't touch it! Polly, how many times to I have to tell you to keep your hands away from your face?"

More than a kajillion? Because she's said it that often. But it's almost impossible not to reach up and touch that thing.

"Is Bridger coming home this weekend? Is he calling tonight?"

"No. Not this weekend. He might call, but it will be late. He's got this study thing on Wednesday nights."

"You think this little dab of leftovers is worth saving? It's not enough for a real meal, is it? I'll just throw it out. Nobody ever wants leftovers."

"Night, Mom."

"Night-night," says Mom, and she steps closer, tucks my hair behind my ear, and squints at the zit. "Make sure you put something on that."

Sometimes homework is interesting, but honestly, I have zero interest left in the fantasy life of W. B. Yeats. Nothing like ten pages, double-spaced, one-inch margins to suck the fun out of an idea. But Ms. Kimmet has already decided I'm going to get an A, so I have to live up to her prejudice. When I hand it in next Monday, it's going to look like something. It's going to have that Polly Furnas sparkle: a companion CD, illustrations, a bibliography in exact MLA style.

The zit is more like an angry little blister, but I scrub the top right off it while I'm exfoliating. It hurts, especially when dab the zit cream on it. I'm probably going to have to use some concealer in the morning.

I wake up because it hurts. Every time my heart beats, my cheek hurts. My eyelashes are glued together with snot. It hurts to touch, but what my fingers feel is worse than hurt. This is wrong, so wrong. "Mom!"

The whole time he's driving us to the hospital, Dad is using his comfort-to-animals voice, "Shhh-sh-sh-sh, there now, there now, shhhh, it's all right . . ."

When we get to the hospital, I see his face in the light streaming out the ER doors. I know something new and horrible. The animal who needs comfort is him.

What doesn't kill it makes it stronger.

That's the story of MRSA.

What doesn't kill it makes it stronger.

They sucked away the pus.

They trimmed away the skin and meat that was dead, that was dying. And deeper and deeper into live flesh, they had to slice that away.

They scraped the bone.

Then they waited. They waited for organ failure. They waited for the flesh to die.

But it didn't.

I didn't.

What doesn't kill it makes it stronger.

But it hurts.

It hurts.

It hurts.

BITCH CREEK:
Almost Anywhere

When I wake up, there's a moment when I almost remember. There was a clock with big, red digital numbers in the exam room. They cut my T-shirt off because it would have hurt to pull it over my head. White tile. Bright lights. The smell of rotting bird. Thing is, lying around in a slightly smelly sleeping bag almost remembering rotting to death gives me no joy.

It's light, it's morning cold, and it's time to stand up and go fishing. It beats the alternative. I unzip the tent and crawl out into the world on my hands and knees. Good morning dirt. Good morning pine needles. Good morning river.

Odd didn't even make it into a sleeping bag. He's immobile in the dirt. It scares me for a minute, but then I can see his back move a little. He's still breathing.

So this stretch of river is mine, for this morning, for this moment. The die-hard early risers are fishing some-place less fished. Easy to reach as it is, this water has been fished and fished to death. The water is as green and dark as wine-bottle glass where it runs deep in the channel, but there are no lunkers lurking there. At my feet the riffle is just thicker air, a gloss over the round rocks of the riverbed. So I might catch nothing. I'm OK with that. Right now, it's just me and the morning and river. I am only that little slice of wind I can whip up with my line. I put this moment, I put this moment, I put this moment—here.

I'm self-medicating. Casting is anesthetic.

When I come back to the campground, Odd is up and sitting hunched beside the fire pit where there is no fire.

"Fuckin' leg hurts," he says. "Every fuckin' thing hurts."

"That's what happens when you sleep on the dirt like a drunk. Get up and move around. Eat some aspirin. Go fishing."

"I don't want to fish. Just get your shit in the car, OK?"

So I do. Ten minutes later my rod is broke down, my tent and sleeping bag are made into bundles, and I'm ready. We drive down the canyon and through a couple piddly-ass towns where half the houses are falling apart and the other half are held together with a fresh coat of paint and some potted geraniums.

We stop for coffee at a place before we hit the interstate. I guess we timed it just right. It is so hot it is impossible to drink. Even doctored up with three tiny cups of Irish Creme and two packs of sugar, it is bitter. I take tiny sips and try not to blister my tongue.

Odd turns on the radio.

I check my phone.

"My dad says you need to call your brother," I say. "You can use mine."

"Piss on that," says Odd.

"OK," I say.

I delete seven messages from Mom. I think she's stopped talking to me. I'm probably in time-out.

We are rolling past the town where Bridger went to university. He's been places here. He's sat in chairs and licked spoons and seen the way the river looks from the bridges in this town. Polly-That-Was was supposed to do those things too, in the future that isn't going to be. Bridger was supposed to take her to movies—and steer her to the easy teachers—and kiss her while they were hiking up to the big M on the side of mountain. That won't be happening. Bridger, that douche, isn't here now. And Polly-That-Was is dead, dead, dead. We don't stop. The interstate blows right by, and so do we.

The back of the tanker is silver and shiny and warps the reflection of D'Elegance's big square grill into a crazy grin. There's a happy, winking cartoon cow painted on there. It's smiling back at D'Elegance and waving a hoof at us. "No BHT!" I guess this should make us happy too.

"Fuckers!" says Odd and hits the steering wheel with both palms.

"What? The trucker? He seems fine. He didn't cut you off or anything."

"Not him. The fuckers with the hormones and antibiotics. He must feel pretty guilty, your dad."

"What?"

"Well, he's there shoving the antibiotics. He probably created the fucking MRSA. He turned some simple crap bug into what ate us."

"That doesn't make sense. I wasn't the first one to get sick. If my dad's work had anything to do with the MRSA, I would have been the first one. I would have been exposed first . . ."

"Don't be stupid. You know it's not like playing tag. I know and you know where it comes from—too many fucking antibiotics—and we know it brews in livestock as good as it does in people. And we know who goes around pumping antibiotics into animals: Your dad."

"My dad isn't the only one."

"That doesn't make it better."

"My dad does not think he did this to me."

"Did you ask him? Did you talk to him?"

I avoided talking about it—not just with my dad. I tried to ignore everything about MRSA. I started going LALA-LALA in my head as soon as I overheard a nurse talking about how the CDC was really interested in this particular strain because it worked so fast—

"It's like Ebola," said the nurse, "but they rot instead of bleed out."

That was the last thing I learned about my MRSA. That was the last thing I wanted to learn about my MRSA.

I never read the obits in paper for Cases One, Two, Four, Five, and Seven. I never visited the chain-link fence by the school where the streaky goodbyes were still written on big sheets of white-painted plywood and where the helmets and shoulder pads of the players who died were rigged up like some gad-awful scarecrows over the football field. After the first trip to the grocery store, I learned to shut my eyes while we drove past. I learned to shut my eye.

After a couple of trips to the grocery store, I learned not to go at all.

People wanted to mourn. They wanted to remember. But they didn't want to be reminded while they were picking out a cantaloupe. They didn't want to glance up and see me touching the bananas. Everybody in town was a MRSA expert by then. They knew how it moves. Everybody in town knew it wasn't like playing tag. It wasn't going to jump through the air into their grocery cart.

Everybody knew it, but they couldn't swallow down the instinctive fear. So I stopped going to town.

It would have been easier on the town if I'd just died too. It would have made the whole thing less random. Random is scary. If a stranger with a gun kills four people, that is way scarier than when four people die in a rollover on the interstate. It's because people die in cars every day. People adjust to the fear, the way deer in a zoo get used to the smell of a tiger. But random is scary.

But I didn't die, I just—randomly—lived.

What if I had died? What would my memorial have been? How would the world remember Polly-That-Was? I didn't belong with the empty-helmet scarecrows. But, then, neither did lunch lady or baby. Was there a wall in the cafeteria where they hung up the lunch lady's picture? Were her ladle and tongs retired? Probably the whole kitchen was gutted and everything she ever touched was incinerated. And the baby? Was it even old enough to have something that it used on purpose? Did its mom ever sit on the floor and cry into a little blanket or a pair of tiny socks?

What about my mom? Could she have lived through it if I died? How would she have remembered Polly-That-Was?

I don't know. I don't want to know. I wouldn't have known.

"I'll find out what's working," says Odd as he pulls in at a casino-cafe-gas-flyshop-saloon. All bases covered, pretty

121

much. He walks toward the flyshop entrance. I guess I'm supposed to wait in the car, but I want the bathroom, so I slink in through a door between the casino and cafe. If I was going to put a bathroom someplace, that would be it.

The sign on the bathroom doors says "Women," but there is also a picture on it. It's a trout dressed up like a saloon-girl in lipstick, mascara, a big purple hat with feathers, and a dress that morphs into a tail. It's a trout. It's a whore. It's every guy's fantasy. And if I step into the bathroom to go pee, I guess I'm buying into it myself. But the other door has a trout wearing a cowboy hat and a gun belt, so there's that.

After I wash my hands, I try to pull my fingers through my hair so I can braid it. It's too late. The back of my head is a prickly mat. I pull a pine needle out of it, but it's a lost cause. I'm a lost cause.

"Free Trout Aquarium," says the sign pointing toward the cafe-giftshop. It might be the only living trout I see all day. Can't pass that up. So I turn my face to the wall and sidle along in the direction the signs lead me.

There's a big trout hovering in a tank that's big enough for it to turn around, but that's it. It's alive, but it probably wishes it wasn't. A fleshy pink wad of something totally wrong is growing on its nose. Do fish get cancer? Is that growth just going to slowly swallow it up? Will they change the sign to "Free Tumor Aquarium"? Then I see the next tank. It is full of smaller trout. One of them, I guess, will grow up and be moved into the front tank and then live out its days in captivity. Free trout my ass. I want to snatch a mass-produced howling wolf-head sculpture and bash it through the glass. I want to scoop up a couple of little trout and run toward the river before they drown in the air.

I'm in a pretty terrible mood when Odd gets back to the car.

"Green Drake, Yellow Sallies, Pale Duns—both morning and evening," says Odd, listing the fly patterns that are working. "You got any of those?"

I just glare at him.

"A Bitch Creek works almost always, so you're set," says Odd. His mood is better than mine, and I hate him for it, big time.

Someone is coming down the path to the river. This is it, I decide. This is the person. This is the place. I'm going to unleash my full-on ugly on this guy—not just my face, but the new deeper-than-skin-deep ugly that is me. I don't have to plan anything. It will be instinctive, like a rattle-snake, because I'm just that full of ugly. It is dripping from my imaginary fangs.

Every step I take up the path I feel stronger, and meaner, and uglier. It feels intensely good.

He's a very old guy. I'm close enough to see that now, he's moving slowly, slowly, down the path. He's using two hiking poles. He's wearing a hat. I might give him a heart attack—

accidentally. If he dies, it will be an act of nature, just like if he slipped off the bank and drowned or hit the trip wire on a coiled snake. I am not responsible for what I am.

"How's the river? How are the trout?" He calls out before I'm ready to engage.

"Can't complain." I keep climbing toward him. I take off my hat. He should be able to see me now . . .

"A beautiful girl on the beautiful river . . ."

What the fuck? Is he fucking blind? One of the hiking poles is slender, white, tipped in red. His eyes are pale and unfocused under the wide brim of his hat. Yes. He is fucking blind—or good as.

The old man starts to talk, but in a moment I know he's not talking, he's reciting. And I remember the words as I hear them. "The Song of Wandering Aengus." I memorized it for my snazzy-dazzle English project.

"I went out to the hazel wood,
Because a fire was in my head,
And cut and peeled a hazel wand,
And hooked a berry to a thread;
And when white moths were on the wing,
And moth-like stars were flickering out,
I dropped the berry in a stream
And caught a little silver trout.

"When I had laid it on the floor
I went to blow the fire aflame,

But something rustled on the floor,
And some one called me by my name:
It had become a glimmering girl
With apple blossom in her hair
Who called me by my name and ran
And faded through the brightening air.

"Though I am old with wandering
Through hollow lands and hilly lands,
I will find out where she has gone,
And kiss her lips and take her hands;
And walk among long dappled grass,
And pluck till time and times are done
The silver apples of the moon,
The golden apples of the sun."

"Yeats," I say.

"Yes, glimmering girl," and he smiles. "Perhaps the world isn't so full of weeping after all."

I don't know if he is talking to me or to himself. He is a very old man. Whatever his eyes see, they do not see me. There is room for me to walk easily past him on the trail while he stares in the direction of the river. The air is still, and I can smell him as I step around him. He smells like an old man. He smells like unwashed clothes and old happiness.

My coiled-up poison is gone.

"We are doomed," says Odd. It's the first thing Odd says when we meet up back at D'Elegance. His good mood was short-lived. I guess he didn't catch anything, but bad fishing is not equal to doom. What now? I don't want to ask. I was feeling pretty good there for a few minutes, and I don't want to lose it because Odd wants to share some sour owl-shit philosophy about how we are all assholes. I just need to redirect his attention. "Hey, I can't think of any monsters that start with E. I'm drawing a blank . . ."

"We are fuckin' doomed," says Odd.

"What you mean? Did we take the wrong turn or something?" I might as well give up and ask. If I don't ask all I'm going to hear for miles will be "doom, doom, doom, doomity, doom, doomed," like a sleepwalking drummer in a marching band. Let's just skip the halftime and get on with the game.

"Something is going to get us," says Odd.

Has he been self-medicating again? With what? Prescription pot isn't supposed to be paranoia-inducing, and what he shared seemed pretty sweet. Maybe catching no fish just gave him too much time to think and work up a mood. A mood of doom.

"We could just crash here for a while and take a nap until you feel better," I say. Naps are golden problem solvers. I learned that at Kid-O-Korral.

"Yeah. Let's just sleep and pretend it's not going to get us."

"Look Odd, we are totally safe. It's a nice day. Nothing

is going to get us. Serial killers are really rare and that parasite . . . just avoid cat boxes. No problem."

"No. Not just us. All of us. Humans are doomed. We are all gonna die."

"You got another headache? I'll buy you some sunglasses and aspirin . . . and coffee and pie. Coffee's good for headaches. It's the caffeine."

"Is caffeine gonna slow down the fucking apocalypse?"

I'm kind of over this conversation. We're all gonna die—blah-blah-blah—what's the point? There is no point—blah-blah-blah. So I try again, "Let's just stop and get some coffee and some pie."

"It's that kind of thinking that makes us doomed."

"Thinking about coffee and pie? How's that deadly?"

"Because it's herd thinking. We all just want to be together and chew pie together and breathe the same air together. It's got to stop."

I agree. Stopping would be good. If we can't stop for coffee and pie, I'd at least like to stop this talking.

"We are all doomed. That is, unless we stay away from the herd and shoot strangers on sight."

"Really, Odd? Shoot strangers on sight? You know that we—you and me—are strangers?"

"If somebody shoots us, it'll serve us right."

It's the last word. He jerks open the car door and slams it after him. He doesn't even wait for me to get in before he starts the engine. I'm useless to him. Conversation over. He leans forward and turns on the radio.

I recognize the song. It's about a little girl with cancer who lost her hair from chemo. I hate that song. I fucking hate the radio. Fuck the rules. I push the scan button.

"This is a fallen world. We live in a fallen world," says the radio.

I push the button again and the radio says, ". . . one of the cars to rupture and leak hydrochloric acid and asphalt into the creek. It is estimated that the three miles below the spill are a dead zone." I imagine the stretch of river I was fishing this morning changed to acid and asphalt, because somewhere that's what happened. I push the button.

". . . more gun violence after all, lefties. Look at Mexico, right? Mexico has gun control. Ciudad Juarez and Culiacan are paradise now! No cartels running around and leaving dead bodies in the middle of the road, right?" I think about the gun at the bottom of the sleeping bag and how useful it would be for killing strangers. Does Odd know where I put it? I hope not.

I have my tiny pair of lucky scissors in my fishing vest. They aren't ordinary fishing scissors meant for tying flies. They are embroidery scissors shaped like a long-beaked bird, a fishing bird. I swiped them out of my mom's jewelry box when I was eleven. They looked lucky and magical, and I figured fishing takes luck so I put them in the pocket of my vest. As far as fishing mojo goes, they do OK. Better than marshmallow hearts and clovers.

Odd is still giving me the silent treatment. He's even turned off the radio.

I dig the little scissors out and start sawing through the mat of hair at the back of my neck. When the hair is in my hand, it's a relief. Less itchy. Less hot. It's an improvement. I could tie a lot of flies, maybe, with a pile of hair like this. I toss the wad of hair out the window. A bird can make a nest out of it, or somebody will mistake it for a chunk of yeti fur. I hack off the hair over my left ear and eye. Then I stop. I leave the tangle on the other side to help hide my ruined cheek.

"Lemme see," says Odd, so I turn toward him. He glances a couple of times, quick, because we are starting up the pass and the road needs attention. "It'll grow back."

It's a start.

"E is for Extras,
Like some monsters got,
Some teeth, mouths, and eyeballs
Where usually there's not."

Odd gives me a bright, full-on smile after he finishes reciting. "There, I did the hard one for you, Polly. Is F for Frankenstein? Or is he too humany for you? One thing you oughta think about is you can break all the rules you want as long as you don't get caught—and nobody's gonna catch *you* because nobody even knows that no-humany-monsters rule except me and you."

"I'll think about that. I'll think about F. Thanks, Odd," I say. He's like my own damn weather: I got to live with it, sometimes it sucks, and it changes every five minutes. Right now the sun is shining on the silky mirror of Lake Coeur d'Alene and there is no wind. There are no clouds in the sky.

"Gotta meditate. You?" says Odd.

"I'm good," I say.

"This'll do then," and he pulls onto an off-ramp to nowhere. He parks D'Elegance in the middle of the road, gets out, walks around the front of the car and starts peeing on the pavement. Because he can, I guess.

When he climbs back in, he's still peeking out of his pants.

"Odd, that's not appropriate. Peeing in public, peeing *on* stuff, not zipping your fly . . ."

He grins and grabs himself, but instead of stuffing himself out of sight, he starts swiveling his penis around like a rubber flashlight. *"Appropriate?"* he says in his Darth Vader voice, "I am the one-eyed god. Who are you, tiny mortal, to tell the one-eyed god what's appropriate? "

"From where I'm sitting, you're the tiny mortal."

He shrugs and the puppet show is over.

EXOTIC MADAME X:

Spokane River

"Look," says Odd, "Thor Street. It's a sign from god. Thor is Troutzilla's right-fin man. We take the next exit."

On a hot day, cold and sweet is very appealing. I'm going to order the hugest drink and suck it down so fast my teeth will ache. This project would have been easier if Odd had just gone to a drive-through, but no, he pulls into a little mall and parks where the signage promises food.

"Need a little change of orientation, body-wise," he says. "Get me a spicy chicken, fries, and Coke." Then he heads toward some little cafe tables that crowd the sidewalk between the street and a coffee house. Lucky me. I get to go in and order. If I weren't so in love with the idea of cold and sweet, I'd just drop the seat back, put my hat over my face, and check out. But I want cold and sweet. I've talked myself into it. I can't live without it.

I put on the granny-Chihuahua sunglasses and pull the brim of my hat down on one side. Then I look in the visor mirror. Krikey. Bad idea, mate. Turns out I can actually make myself look worse. Well, maybe not worse, but more obvious. Obvious isn't good. Shit. I'm a person. I can buy lunch in public. I toss the sunglasses in the back seat and restore dignity to my hat. Then I walk into a place that promises fast, fresh, Mexican food. They don't have a spicy chicken sandwich or fries on the menu. That is just fine with me.

When I come out with the food, Odd isn't where I saw him last. He's table-hopped so he's sitting near a girl with a black umbrella shading her from the sun. Not an umbrella, a parasol with ruffles and ribbons. Not a parasol, a gothasol. She's a goth. A real live and beautiful goth: hair as black as ebony, skin as white as snow, lips as red as. . . .

"She eats raw fish. I'm not talkin' sushi, I'm talkin'—like Gollum," says Odd when I walk over. He mimes a sharp-toothed monster gnawing the guts out of a trout.

The gothasol girl dabs the end of a fry in the pool of ketchup. She dabs it slowly, in and out, in and out. Then she drops it into the pool and pushes it away. She blots her fingertips on a paper napkin to remove any trace of oil or salt. Her manners are impeccable. It must be hell keeping that satin corset clean. It would be for me, anyway.

I dressed up like a goth for the Halloween dance freshman year.

That was the dance where Bridger noticed me—like, *really* noticed me and said my name and danced with me. When he put his hand on the low part of my back, my insides zinged and tingled and ached. Just being close to him was that good. And, even though wearing a T-shirt that says "This IS my costume" is sort of lame, I was grateful he wasn't dressed like a zombie or wearing a Scream mask because I could see his face. When he smiled his teeth looked purply white under the black lights.

I felt like Cinderella—scared that when the dance was over I'd be so ordinary he'd never notice me again. When I was at Chrissie's house getting ready for the dance we had howled about how hilarious we looked. We painted on super-gory red lipstick and big black wings of eyeliner. We tottered around on ridiculously high and pinchy shoes. Basically, we looked like breathing Bratz dolls. We were bendable and posable and hoochied up. So I was afraid that I would not be nearly so interesting when he saw me in daylight in jeans and sneaks.

But Monday came and Bridger cared enough to find out where my locker was and give me a ride home. In less than a week we skipped right past talking to loving each other forever. And we meant it—at the time.

Now I'm sitting across from this girl, a real live goth, and I have to face facts. She got up this morning and put plenty of effort into how she looks. Her hair is clean and arranged in perfect ringlets cascading down the side of her neck. Her fingernails are not just clean; they are lovely squared ovals of matte black with glossy red moons. She smells like perfume: lilacs with a hint of patchouli and a base note of rubber.

I've been wearing the same fishing shorts and ripped *South Park* T-shirt for six days. I don't smell—I reek. I probably distort the light waves with my BO.

One of us is a social misfit and a weirdo. It ain't her.

I put the drinks and bag of food on the table and take the chicken burrito I bought for Odd out of the bag and put it in front of him.

I pick up my paper bag full of tacos and one giant vat of soda, sweating cold on the outside.

"I'm going to the car," I say, "I'll eat there."

It's not posh, but it's a place with a bed and a shower. I told Odd that I'm tired of sleeping rough, but the truth is I just feel dirty. I am dirty. I am layers of dirty stuck together with sweat and wood smoke and sunscreen and DEET.

The mirrors in the hotel are screwed down tight against the wall. There's one over the dresser. There's another over the double sinks. There's a third full-length one on the back of the bathroom door. Can anybody want to see herself that often? I don't. I shut the curtains and turn off the lights and crank up the air conditioner.

Odd gets the shower first. He's got plans. The gothasol told him about places. He is going to those places.

Goodbye, Odd. Good luck with that. Don't let the door flatten your skinny ass on the way out.

I peel off my clothes, and after being in the same things 24-7 for so long, peeling is the truth. I passed a coin-op washer and dryer in an alcove down the hall near the ice machine, but I wouldn't have anything to wear while I washed my wardrobe unless I wrapped a sheet around me like a toga. I'm just not up for the costume party. I throw the clothes in bottom of the tub and turn on the shower.

The water is hot—so hot it's going to be bad for my skin, as I recall from the lessons of lady-TV. I should avoid harsh bar soap like the little munchkin cake stamped with the name of the hotel. I should use a gentle cleanser and gentle circular strokes with the tips of my fingers. I rub soap on a washcloth and scrub. After I rinse, I can feel the dead skin rolling up into little balls. So I attack my face again until it stings like a rug burn. Harsh soap and hot water will give me premature crow's feet. Well, crow's foot, actually, ladies. What is your advice regarding lumpy red scar tissue? A greenish tinted concealer to counteract the redness . . . and avoid . . . being seen?

Odd used all the shampoo in the little bottle. Not a surprise. I scrub everything with the soapy washcloth, even what's left of my Raggedy Ann hair, which feels all yarny and looks like it was knit onto my head and then styled by fat little preschool fingers using round-nosed safety scissors. Lather, rinse, repeat. And repeat. And repeat.

A good thing about hotel showers in the middle of the afternoon is that the hot water is endless. I might just stay here until I mutate into a drowned half-mermaid zombie with pruney white fingers. My clothes are underfoot. Every time I step I'm stomping the sudsy runoff and squishing out the dirt. I will not smell bad. I will smell like soap. I pick up each piece and hold them over the showerhead until they are rinsed, rinsed, rinsed. I turn my back, wring out as much water as I can and then flip the wet things over the shower-curtain rod. When I'm done with the laundry, I just stand there and feel the water sluicing down my back.

It's going to take time for them to dry. I turn off the shower, but I promise to come back soon. Then I roll my shirt and panties in a towel and wring and squeeze. Still wet, of course. Just outside the bathroom door is an iron and ironing board. I plug in the iron and start pressing my T-shirt. It still looks a little grotty, but the rising steam smells clean. Pretty soon only the seams are damp. I pull the shirt over my head and take a couple swipes at my panties. Presto. Good enough. I hang my socks and shorts up on the coat hangers. They will be dry by morning. Then I slide into the bed. The sheets feel clean. The pillows are too big, too good. The air conditioner purrs on, and I have nothing to do but sleep.

I could have slept a lot longer if Odd hadn't showed up again.

Apparently the gothasol hadn't taken the meeting to be a hard-and-fast arrangement, because she never showed. I don't blame her. Odd clings to the notion that something must have come up.

I make a pillow sandwich around my head. This doesn't keep Odd from talking. He doesn't really need any response. I wish I really couldn't hear him.

"Hey. Wanna fuck?"

"Shit no!"

"Well I do. It would be the perfect end to a pretty good day."

"Not good enough. You got two hands and I bet you know how to take care of your own. But I'd appreciate it if you were a little discreet."

"It's my leg, isn't it? You can't get past that? Right?"

I can't believe what I'm hearing.

"You are one cold, mean bitch. I mean, have you looked at *yourself*?"

It's like the words flip a switch in the back of my brain.

"Look, Odd, I am not having sex with you. It isn't because of your leg. It is because I don't want to. That's it. Whole story. If you had your leg, I still wouldn't want to, because you are an asshole."

He chews on that for thirty seconds. This is not the first time he's heard that he's an asshole, so he processes the info pretty fast. He picks up the clicker and turns on the TV. ESPN . . . CNN . . . some enthusiastic chirper selling jewelry. . . . "For videos to suit your adult desires, press menu now. There's always something new," says the TV.

"So can we watch some porn?"

"Traveling with kids? Press guest services to block adult content," says the TV.

"Forget it, Odd. I'm not paying for porn."

After a few more clicks of the remote, he stops.

I can now chart Odd's hierarchy of desires, just like I learned to do in Psychology/Social Studies/Elective:

1) Sex with someone attractive.
2) Sex with anyone, even me.
3) Porn on TV.
4) Watching a guy fail to truck surf.

I just want coffee, but Odd wants breakfast. Drive-through won't do. He wants to sit in a booth. I do not. I give him a twenty and tell him bring me coffee. Then I drop the seat back and settle out of sight.

"Hey, open it. My hands'r full."

Odd is standing there with a giant to-go cup of coffee and a pie. No. Not pie. It's in an aluminum pie pan, but it is covered with whipped topping and a dozen whole peanut butter cups. That is not pie. Odd hands it to me and slides into the driver's seat. He offers me the coffee. The lid isn't on tight. It's too damn hot to hold, but there's no good place to put it. I slide the pie-thing onto my lap. Now at least I can shift the coffee from hand to hand.

"I could lean over and eat that pie, Polly," Odd says. "Mmmm. Pie." He makes snorting, slobbery noises.

"Zip it, Odd. And keep your talking trout puppet in your pants."

"So what happens in a brain that leads to three life-size fiberglass Holsteins sailing a red boat in a field?" I ask.

"What?" says Odd. He's steering with his left hand. His right hand is full of pale chocolate pudding and whipped topping.

"Right back there. Three cows in a boat. You would have seen it if you were paying attention instead of sucking down pie by the handful."

"I'm paying attention to the *road*," says Odd, "I can't be staring out the window."

"The *road's* out the window."

"No, the road's out the *windshield*. I know where it is because I'm looking at it," says Odd, licking his palm and reaching for more glop.

"UFO," says Odd.

"What?"

"UFO. Un-i-fucking-dentified flying object. Right there, coming up," says Odd. And it is. There is a rusty flying saucer on top of a little hill. How do three cows end up in a boat? I'm pretty sure the answer is related to the thought, "I'm gonna weld me up a flying saucer and put it on the hill."

"My leg hurts so fucking much," says Odd. He reaches over and wipes his hand on my clean shirt like I'm a napkin. Then he reaches toward his robot leg. Toward the place where nothing should hurt anymore, but it does.

The trees thin out, then they disappear. Knobs of rotten black rock jut out of the hills. Basalt, like in Yellowstone, decaying into ragged teeth. It's hard country, but there's water. There are people fishing.

"Pull over."

"No, it's a cardigan, but thanks for noticing."

"Just take the next exit, Odd."

"The lady needs to pee again? What are you? A camel?"

"The lady needs to fish."

"Alrighty then."

I'm about to leave Odd behind on the bank and go to the next good place when he gets lucky on his first cast. That's something. I figure I'll stick around to watch the fun, maybe help with the net, because this one looks like it's big enough to require that sort of thing.

At that moment, there is a buzz. A distinctive and unwelcome buzz. And then WHAM! A snake hits Odd right in the robot leg. Odd reacts, BAM! And lashes out with the rod in his hand—because that's what is in his hand. It's a bad idea. The rod shatters. The snake recoils. Odd just flings himself off the bank. It was probably meant to be a jump, but it's more of a collapse. But the next strike falls short, so that's mission accomplished. And the snake disappears. It doesn't want be involved in this, either.

"You OK?"

"Fuckin' snake bit me. It bit me."

I worry I saw wrong. Maybe it didn't just hit metal then. Maybe it hit meat.

"Come on. We'll get you to the car. We'll get you help. Does it hurt?"

"No. It doesn't hurt. The fuckin' thing doesn't hurt at all now," says Odd, and he whacks his robot leg with what's left of his rod. "I. Can't. Feel. A. Fuckin'. Thing." Each word is another slash with the butt of the broken rod. Then he chucks the ruined handle and reel out into the lake. He picks up a rock.

"No! Stop!" I grab his hand and put my other arm over the robot leg. If he starts pounding on it with the rock, he could do some damage. He lets go of the rock. He lets me take it. He's not angry. He's not scared. He's not even sad.

"Do you want me to try to find your reel? I can probably just follow the line."

"Don't. I don't need it. I don't want it. What's the point? I can't catch nothing but the MRSA."

He opens up the passenger side, gets in, and slams the door.

I break down my rod and get everything in order. Then I just sort of wait for Odd to move into the driver's seat. He needs to get over being rattled.

Then he leans over and pops the driver's-side door open. Maybe he needs to talk. So I walk over and get in the car. I feel like a little kid sitting there. The seat is too far back.

I remember playing in Dad's truck, kneeling on the seat so I could see out. "Never touch the gearshift, Polly," says Dad. And of course I did. And of course the truck started rolling down the slope into the herd of cattle my dad had come to take care of—until the front tires slipped into a little ditch. My mouth banged hard on the steering wheel and my teeth cut through my lip. I'd only just started crying when Dad jerked the door open. He was mad for a moment, and then he scooped me up and said, "Don't cry, Polly. It's OK. It's OK. It's just a little blood. It won't leave a scar."

"Hey, it's OK," I start the conversation.

"Shut up and drive," says Odd.

"You're OK, aren't you? The snake didn't really bite you, right? There's no emergency. When you are ready to go, we'll go."

"Gimme a break. Just drive."

I don't say anything. I just point at the lump of blind scar.

"Bullshit," says Odd, "You can see fine out of your left eye. Just drive, you pussy."

So I'm creeping down the blacktop slowly, so slowly, slow as a little old man wearing a hat, and we all know how slow they drive. I hate it. I hate driving. I hate being half blind. I hate Odd. I hate big two-fisted trout that won't be caught. I hate Bridger, too, a lot, as long as I'm at it.

I hate everything so much that I turn around after a while and find my way back to the interstate. I wait at the top of the merging ramp until I can't see another car or truck in any direction, and then I'm driving toward Portland by way of Kennewick. The green sign says so. I'm not going fast, but I'm driving. And, honestly, I might be a better driver than that pie-scarfing emo-coaster Odd Estes.

On a straight stretch I reach out and turn on the radio, because the driver calls the tune, and, hey! It's me, the driver.

... "Don't think of them as preowned. It's a new car with a few miles on it, just a little bit of experience on the road." Under the car salesman's voice I hear the question: who wants a virgin car?

... accordion music and Spanish. So what's with that anyway? Are those songs really all dark and full of drug-war drama? Can lyrics about machine-gunning people really be set to accordion music? I'm sure not knowing, but hey, polka 'or waltz? And waltz is the wrong answer so ... KAPOW! Stranger things have happened, I guess.

... "We live in a fallen world. This is a fallen world ..."

... "... guys we go after are the guys who have already screwed up an NCAA scholarship ..." Odd turns up the volume. I bat his hand away, driver calls the tune, Odd, you douche bag, and I'm driving.

... "'... her right to cover her face if she wants to ...'

'No, not in America.'

'Isn't it a personal freedom? Isn't that what America's about?'

'There's nothing free about making women cover up their faces. There is nothing free about that.'

'But if it's a woman's own choice? Isn't it her choice to decide if she's going to wear a veil?'

'There are lots of laws about what a person can wear. Laws about decency. And this is really about decency. There's something indecent about covering up your face. Criminals do it. How would you feel if a guy walks into a convenience store with a ski mask on? We have the right to see the people around us ...'

'This is different. This is her religion. This is part of who she is. She's not going to rob any convenience store ...'

'How do you know? She could be hiding a bomb under that sack that covers her up from her head to her toes.'

'It's a niqab. It has a name ...'

'Maybe her religion tells her to blow people up. I think her freedom of religion stops before she gets to commit terrorism ...'

'Look, we aren't talking about terrorism. We are talking about a woman's right to dress according to her
beliefs . . . when she takes her children to school,
when she goes to the store to buy groceries.'

'She can do whatever she wants in her own home, in
her own—whatever they call their churches—but
when she's in public she has to respect the rights
of others. Respect the ways of America.'

'Her ways are American, too. She's an American too.'"

And then it's time for station identification and the
pledge-drive pitch. I don't want a mug. I don't want a tote.
I want to know if a Vagina American has the right to cover
her face. I turn off the radio.

"So what do you think, Odd?"

"I think we need gas," he says.

I look at the gauge. He's right, but that's not what I was
asking. "OK. I'll stop at the next place. Help me watch for
the signs. But Odd, I was wondering, is it OK for Muslim
women to wear veils in public?"

"Huh?"

And I get it. He hasn't been listening. Not giving a shit
is a two-way street. I don't give a shit about football, and he
doesn't give a shit about *niqabs*. He's not a Vagina American. He's not a Muslim. The only time he cares about a
face mask is if there is a penalty that moves the chains.

THE MODIFIED UNICORN:
The Middle of Nowhere

I keep driving, but I wonder: Who gets to decide what's decent and indecent? Who gets to decide? Why does my face need to be naked but my boobs need to be not? Why is Odd's one-eyed trout puppet way out of line? Would an eye patch make me a pirate? Would a baggy dress make me a terrorist?

"Hey, that sign says gas next right," says Odd. So I take the off-ramp, but wherever we are going, wherever the gas is, isn't here. Not right here. The question is, do I trust what I see, which is vast tracts of nothing, or what the sign promised? Either way we are going to be out of gas pretty soon. There's a whole lot of the world I can't see. So I keep driving down the two-lane and pretty soon I do see something. Not a town, but a lot of busted-up machinery, rusted combines and snowplows and caterpillar tractors. It looks like I've found a place where those things go to die.

Next thing you know, I'm in a sort of one-street town. This town looks deader than Elkhorn, to be honest. But there's a gas station. Looks vacant, but the door opens when we push it and there's a guy sitting on a stool behind the counter.

The pumps are old, so cash is good. When I ask about the bathroom, the guy waves in the direction of the store just down the street. There isn't even a cat or a dog anywhere. Faded banners hang from the streetlights. This is the home of the Combine Demolition Derby, according to the banners. That explains a lot. Once a year, people come here to watch big machines in a slow-dance cage match. Then, when it's over, the broken machines just sit there and rust. This is not the weekend when that happens, so nothing is happening. Unless you count machines dissolving into rust, because that is happening, that is always happening. While I go pee in the little bathroom, I think I'm rusting too. I'm dissolving into blood and pee and sweat and tears. A demolition derby is probably the best thing I can hope for. I flush the toilet and splash water on my face.

There isn't much that's appetizing on the shelves, but I grab a warm six-pack of root beer, a box of crackers, and a jar of peanut butter. The woman at the counter looks a little beat down and bored. She sets the book she's reading pages-down on the counter by the cash register. It's a romance. I will never look like the half-dressed girl on the cover. I look at the woman ringing up my crackers. She's never going to look like the girl on that cover either. I hand her the money. She hands me my change. She picks up the paperback before I pick up the bag of food. She doesn't seem that enthusiastic, but it's hard to tell. She just seems so bored. Neither of us has a said a word to the other.

When I get in the Caddie, Odd says, "You wanna stick around here for a few days?"

Is he that excited about farm equipment destruction? Does he want to see a thresher get thrashed? Well, of course he does. How many days is it to the big event, anyway?

"If we stay until Thursday we can enter the cribbage tournament," says Odd, "The prize is a box of meat. I saw it on the gas station bulletin board. How 'bout that? A box of meat!" His smile at me proves he thinks that's kind of funny. He's standing by the passenger-side door. I guess I'm still driving. Hey, that's something. I'm a driving person again. It isn't a box of meat, but it's something. I'm moving my story down the road.

We're eating a picnic of saltines and peanut butter washed down with root beer and vodka. It's a pretty messed-up meal.

"You know, Polly, if you'd had the gun you coulda shot that snake," says Odd.

"No way I could have shot that snake even if I wanted to, and why should I want to? It was just defending itself. Live and let live," I say. That's pretty much the line I've heard my whole life about snakes.

"Don't think you'd be so liberal if it was you that got bit," says Odd.

"Well, it didn't really bite *you*," I say.

"This is my goddamn leg and this is the goddamn leg it bit," says Odd.

"Well, even if I did want to kill a snake, no way could I have shot it. Snake is like *this* wide," I hold up a cracker, "And that wouldn't be easy to hit." I eat the cracker and take a nice deep swallow of the vodka in the flask. There's not that much left. This picnic is probably the last of the vodka— then we'll have to resort to what's left of the whiskey. Unless Odd decides to rob another liquor store.

"You just need practice," says Odd, "That's a situation that can be rectified." He takes a handful of crackers and walks across the road and sticks a couple of crackers and a root-beer can on the top of a big black fence post. "Get the gun."

Well, sure, why not? We're a gazillion miles from anywhere, and we have more peanut butter than vodka. Might as well shoot some poor innocent saltines. Better that than a snake.

Odd pays me no mind while I rummage down into my sleeping bag for the sock full of gun and the sock full of bullets. He's just leaning against the grill of the car and staring off into the wide nothing wheat fields and the wide nothing sky. I load before I walk back to the front of D'Elegance.

"See that, right there? Those crackers are my brother Buck's balls," says Odd.

The first shot doesn't even hit anything as far as I can see. The second hits something, because the can and crackers fly off and land in front of the fence post.

We walk over to visit scene of the crime. There's no bullet hole in the can. The crackers are busted, but if one of them had taken a direct hit it seems like it would be blown to smithereens.

"Here it is," says Odd. The bullet hole isn't that obvious because the post is stained black with creosote.

"You would have killed him," I say and point to the hole. "Would have hit his femoral artery."

"The target's not exactly anatomically correct," says Odd, "Although Buck is a dickhead." Odd picks up the root-beer can and props a couple more crackers up against it. "Well, Polly, who you gonna shoot?"

"I thought I was just shooting imaginary snakes," I say.

"I thought you weren't a snake shooter," says Odd.

"I'm not a people shooter, either," I say.

"You sure about that? 'Cause I think you might find it relaxing to shoot somebody who needs shot."

"Doesn't seem right . . ."

"Polly, it's a can and some crackers . . ."

"OK. I'm going to shoot Bridger."

"Atta girl," says Odd, "It'll do you good."

I walk back and rest my butt steady on the car. Then I lift the gun and fire. The can and crackers are still there. I hold the gun with both hands, steady, and fire again; I take a step and fire again, I'm almost on top of the damn target and CRACK, I finally get some satisfaction. The can bounces to the dirt. I put the gun down carefully on the other side of the fence and then shimmy between the lines of barbed wire. I pick up the gun and walk up to the can. I turn the gun sideways like they do on TV when the shooter is badass. I put another bullet into Bridger. And another. And another.

"Alrighty then, that can's pretty darn dead, Polly. You can stop," says Odd. He holds the wires of the fence apart, which is thoughtful. And he's right about the shooting. I feel very relaxed. Then he reaches for the gun. His hands, I notice for the first time, are so much bigger than my hands. Big, like the paws of a puppy. He takes the gun and pumps one more round into Bridger, or the can that is Bridger's heart.

"I'm with you, Polly," he says.

When I look at him, his dark pupils almost swallow his gray eyes. I can feel my eye open, too, and the bottom falls out of my world. But then I shake my head . . . no, no, no. He's just a puppy, but I don't know who I'm talking to, him or me, but the answer is no. I don't know if I said no to love or to murder. I just don't.

We sit on the hood of the car, leaning up against the windshield. It's pretty comfortable once a person moves the windshield wipers up and out of the way. To the east the sky is turning lavender and gray; to the west it is simmering orange.

"We ought to pitch the tents while we can still see to do it. We'll be lucky if we can find a level patch," I say.

"I'm not sleeping in no tent," says Odd.

"OK, I guess it doesn't look like it'll rain. It's going to be a starry night."

"I'm sleeping in D'Elegance. Snakes," says Odd.

"That snake is a hundred miles away," I say.

"Not the only snake in the world. I been bit once today. That's plenty for me," says Odd.

"Look once you get in the tent and zip it up, no snakes can get inside . . ."

"So they just wait until I unzip it to get up and take a leak, then BAM. Probably get me right in the face—or worse. I don't need that."

"I never heard of that happening in my whole life," I say.

"So what? You're bearanoid, and you never got attacked by a bear. I can be crazy about snakes if I wanna be," says Odd.

"That backseat isn't even comfortable for me, and I'm a lot shorter than you."

"I'll just recline the front seat. That's comfortable as hell," says Odd.

"So you're never going to sleep in a tent again?"

"Not in no place full of snakes I'm not," says Odd, "but I might invent me a portable snake fence a person could put around a tent. Be about an inch high and electrified. A person'd have to be careful about taking a leak, though, with a system like that."

Neither of us moves to pitch a tent. The night seeps across the sky, but the air is still warm and there aren't any mosquitoes. The stars creep out, one a time, a handful at a time, until the sky is full.

When I put away the peanut butter and crackers, I hide the gun again. I think for a moment about finding a new place, but I like having it close it when I'm asleep. There is no better place than snug inside a bloody sock. My housekeeping is done. I check my phone. The screen glows bright in the dark; the letters are little dark stars on a bright sky.

From Dad: "Odd shd call brother now."

From Mom: sixteen messages I don't read.

"Scootch down for a sec," I say when I bring my sleeping bag back to the front of the car. "We can share . . ." It's way too warm to climb into a sleeping bag, but it feels really comforting to use it like a big, flat pillow over the glass and metal. "So," I say when I get settled, "your brother is still waiting for a call."

"Piss on that," says Odd.

"Any particular reason you want to, like . . . shoot him in the balls? I thought you were . . . proud? of him. He's on the radio . . ."

"Piss on that," says Odd.

"Shooting star," I say.

"You can see pretty good with that one eye," says Odd.

"I can see the stars. I can watch TV. I can thread the eye of hook."

"You can drive."

"I can," I say. "Seeing is going OK. Being seen still sort of sucks."

"Well, Polly, you look OK to me," says Odd. It's dark and he's staring at the sky, but it's a thoughtful gesture.

"I still don't know why you want to shoot Buck," I say after a while.

"Two words: Truck Nutz."

"What?"

"Truck Nutz. Plastic balls—stupid prick's still swinging a pair off the back hitch of his truck. That's his mentality. He's a prick. He's been raining shit on me since I can remember. If you had a brother, you might not have to ask."

"What I said about being an only child. That's not exactly true. I might have a bunch of brothers and sisters. My mom put them all up for adoption a few years ago," I say. "They were snowflake babies. You know what those are, Odd? Leftover fertilized eggs. They freeze them. They can last for years, just waiting for somebody to thaw them out so they can start growing."

"Weird," says Odd.

"Tell me about it. For all I know one of my little brothers or sisters is being born right now, tonight." And I think about how that is. How it is to be born. I don't remember that. I don't think my mom even remembers that, because she told me about seeing me for the first time and how I looked bigger than her leg and she couldn't really believe I had come out of her . . . they swooped in and took me away . . . she met me again in the NICU, the newborn intensive unit . . . she couldn't touch me because I was under a hard plastic bubble full of oxygen until I stabilized . . . and other babies were there with gauze over their eyes and wires attached to their brains . . . and Mom told me one had a card on his incubator that said "Shawn the Man" . . . but he was not bigger than a can of pop . . . and she was so frightened until the nurse came and said, "This one's strong. She wants to live." . . . and I did.

"So your mom sold her eggs?"

"Nope. My mom *bought* the eggs from a student who needed tuition money. That's the story. My mom bought eggs from a red-haired girl who was really smart and needed money for graduate school. Mom put an ad in university papers and she offered extra money for high SAT scores. Then those eggs got fertilized and I was one of them and I was born. And after a while my mom read about how people wanted to adopt "snowflakes"—these frozen embryos—so she put them up for adoption. We had a family meeting about it, but it was basically Mom's deal."

"So these frozen babies, they're like your clones? That is fucked up nine ways from Sunday, Polly."

"What's so fucked up about it?"

"You could meet some guy and marry him and never know he was your brother. That's one fucked-up thing, marrying your own clone," says Odd.

"I can think of a few reasons why that won't happen. And they aren't clones—they are more like brothers and sisters—we'll be similar, but not exactly alike. Like you and Buck."

"I'm nothing like Buck," says Odd.

"And those snowflake babies are probably nothing like me," I say. "They're just out there, maybe, even though I don't know where."

"My sister Thea's like that," says Odd. "She left for Reno three years ago because she was tired of Dad and Buck ragging on her. She was going to learn how to deal poker, but the last time she called she told my mom she was working as a security guard in the Meadowood Mall."

"Her plans changed. She just adapted to her new condition," I say.

"I miss her sometimes," says Odd.

"I don't miss my brothers and sisters," I say, "I don't know how to miss them."

"I'm going to bed—I mean, I'm going to car," says Odd. "You want me to turn on the headlights so you can pitch your tent?"

"I think I'll just sleep in the other seat. I'll come to bed in a while."

My eye can see the sky, empty and full of stars. My eye is cryogenically frozen and sees nothing, not even the dark. I am an only child who has lots of brothers and sisters. My mother is in the kitchen back home, wiping the sink until it shines just like she does every night. My mother is an egg donor I have never seen. My mother loves me so much it drives both of us crazy. My mother sold me to pay bills.

"F is for frozen
Much colder than snow,
Seeds of little monsters
Are waiting to grow.

"And I did a new one for C," I say. "Like you said, 'C is for creatures' was really not my best work."

"C is for cephalopod,
A nightmare-soaked squid
In the folds of your brain
Where it always stays hid."

"You know, Polly, I would maybe like not to have monsters in my brain before I go to sleep. Know what I mean? Like, couldn't you just say goodnight?"

"Goodnight, sleep tight, don't let the bedbugs bite . . ."

"No bugs, Polly. And don't say one word about snakes while you're at it. I don't want snakes in my head."

"You're the one who brought up snakes. What do you want? Unicorns?"

"Blowjobs are good."

"OK. Dream about blowjobs and unicorns."

"That'll work. I think maybe that goth girl is gonna be riding on that unicorn. G'night, Polly."

"G'night."

G is for Gothasol
To keep out the light,
Riding a unicorn:
You hope she won't bite.

TROUT CHOW:

Bonneville Hatchery

Here they put the trees in straitjackets. Here the clouds are stacked like mountains and drag their black shadows over the green fields. This bridge is called the Blue Bridge. It is almost but not quite the color of the sky I can see between the beams of the . . .

"Fuck!" Odd jerks the steering wheel and moves us away just before the driver's-side mirror and the curving silver mirrored tank of the semi are in the same place at the same time. "Fuck, Polly! Fuck! Fuck!"

My hands are tight on the steering wheel now. My eye is trying to see everything dangerous at once. There is no sky. There is cement and metal and huge black tires that could eat D'Elegance whole. The trailer fishtails a little and then it moves in front of us. It is very shiny. The winking cow. Got Milk. No BHT. We are off the bridge. Traffic lights. Merging lanes. Parked cars.

"Pull over, Polly, now!"

I do it. Suddenly D'Elegance is parked halfway on a sidewalk, but at least the world isn't flying at me so fast.

"I'll drive now," says Odd. He isn't angry. He isn't even scared anymore. He is just matter-of-fact.

I nod and fumble with the seat belt.

"Alrighty then," says Odd, and he adjusts the rearview mirror before he backs out into a gap in the traffic.

We stop for gas at the edge of town. I clean every window on D'Elegance twice—dripping sponge, squeegee, dripping sponge, squeegee. I wash the big, square headlamps.

Odd stands and watches. I'm pretty sure he doesn't see the point. I just don't know how else to apologize to the car. I put D'Elegance in harm's way. She's been good to me, and I shouldn't have treated her like that.

Odd's side of the world is made of cliffs. My side of the world is made of river. Both sides of the world are dotted in the distance with white towers and the pinwheel blades of wind turbines.

The radio is on and I'm half listening to it, ". . . very large mountain lion sitting in a tree in the backyard . . . dispatched the cougar without injury to any humans or pets in the area . . . probably means that the cougar was destroyed . . . my wife has told to me quit admitting when I make mistakes . . . I am not anti-yard sale . . . an underground economy . . . that's not derogatory . . . in 1910 William Howard Taft signed the White Slave Traffic Act, which made it illegal to transport women across state lines for immoral purposes . . ."

"Why exactly am I transporting you across state lines, Polly?"

Sometimes the best thing to say to Odd is to punch him, so I do.

"Bridge of the Gods, Polly. Guy at the gas station said to make sure to see the Bridge of the Gods. Said if you run on it, there's an optical illusion and the bridge disappears. Said it works best if a person gets in the right frame of mind."

This is why we are sitting in a parking lot, staring at the impressive pile of cement needed to defy gravity and hold up a two-lane bridge across the Columbia River. It's Odd's plan. We are fulfilling step one: get in the right frame of mind. His prescription, as it turns out, is part of the plan. And the last little bit of the vodka in the red aluminum flask. Also helpful.

There is a mural painted on the cement. A picture of the once-upon-a-time Bridge of the Gods, which was a natural bridge that reached from Oregon to Washington—at least, that's what the mural shows. The rock bridge fell down, and now there is this replacement bridge made of metal and cement.

"Come on Polly, let's go take a look," says Odd, and he climbs out to D'Elegance like closer inspection of the faded, scabby painting is worth it. I follow because maybe it is. Can't get disappointed if I don't give it a try.

They say there was a land bridge and humans followed the wooly mammoths over from Siberia, so I suppose it's possible that there could have been a stone arch that reached all the way across this river. I got my doubts. I always have my doubts.

"Hey Polly, it's Lewis and Clark," Odd has gone round to one of the side of the cement wall. When I follow him, I see them. Lewis and Clark. There are standing on top of a pile of transportation options—steamboats, trains, a car—which is kind of funny since they didn't have access to any of that when they hauled their sorry asses to the Pacific and back. Maybe the paint is just faded, but they look like statues instead of people. It's all about the heroic pose. Odd can spend more time staring than I can, so I wander around to the other side. This side is devoted to wildlife. Eagle, bear, wolf, mountain lion with crazy eyes: it's a stack of predators with nothing to eat.

"Where's the fish?" I ask. "Did you see fish? There are no fish in this picture."

"Relax, Polly. You'll get your fish. Next stop after this is the dam and the fish hatchery," says Odd, "Besides, I got a feeling we might see Troutzilla himself once we get out onto the bridge."

"How'd he get here all the way from Butte?" I'm feeling a little fuzzy-headed and cotton-mouthed.

"Not Troutzilla the monster—Troutzilla the god. Stands to reason a person might see Troutzilla the god from the Bridge of the Gods," says Odd, "And also, there's the optical illusion." With that, he heads out of the parking lot toward the bridge. I don't want to follow. I'm not liking the idea of walking across this bridge. If I face the oncoming traffic the cars will be passing on my blind side. If I walk with my back to the traffic, cars will be coming up behind me. There is no way I can feel safe.

There is a tollbooth. I don't even go close enough to hear how much it costs, but Odd is waving his arms like he does when he's being friendly with strangers.

"Come on, Polly!"

When he calls, I duck my head down and slink past the toll station like a dog.

There's no sidewalk. We'll be sharing the lane with loaded trucks and speeding cars—and bicycles, oh, sure, just throw bicycles into the mix. A train is coming. It crosses under the road. I can't hear; I can't see. Perfect hell. Odd paid money to walk me straight into perfect hell.

Then it gets worse.

The pavement ends. The bridge is nothing but metal mesh and air. I take a couple of steps and then, "I can't do this!" I turn back.

Before I get away, Odd catches up, grabs my hand, and says, "Come on, Polly. It's great. I promise."

"It's not fun, Odd. I'm scared. I think I'm going to throw up. You go . . . check it out."

"It won't be fun without you," says Odd.

"That's dumb," I say.

"It might be dumb, but it's true." He's giving me the full-on sad puppy.

"It makes me dizzy when I look down."

"Don't look down."

"If I don't look down, I can't see if I'm safe from traffic. There's no way this is going to work," I say.

"You just hold my hand, and I'll do all the watching. You can look at my back or you can shut your eyes. Once you get out there a ways, you'll see. It's worth it," says Odd. He still hasn't let go of my hand. When he pulls me gently toward the bridge, I follow. After a hundred steps, I open my eye and look down. I can see birds flying under my feet, but I do not see Troutzilla. I see Odd. He's smiling.

"You want to visit the dam or the hatchery?" asks the security guard on duty.

"Um, I thought they were both here," says Odd.

"They are, but you go that way for the hatchery and this way for the dam." The guard points. The road to the dam is blocked with a yellow-and-black-striped traffic gate. "You're free to visit the dam," says the guard, "But there is a security check and some areas are restricted."

I wonder if this guy and his gate could stop a terrorist. Or a pirate.

"I just want to see some fish," I say.

"Alrighty then, hatchery it is," says Odd.

When I check my phone, I have a message from my dad, "Call odds brother."

"Im on it all good," I tell Dad.

I delete thirty-three messages from Mom.

We didn't come at the right time to see the live spawning activity, but there is a looping video of fish porn in the big white building. All salmon die after spawning, says the film, but they are humanely euthanized prior to the artificial spawning process. The fish are bigger than my arm, silver and limp, when they are removed from the anesthetic tank. They are stunned with electroshocks. Electrocution kills the pain, I guess. Is it more humane than whacking them with a rock? It's tidier, anyway. Human hands grasp and bend the males and the milt pours out, streams of rich milk into a bucket. Human hands slit the girl fish right up the tender white underbelly and empty out the eggs. The valuable eggs. Then they toss the empty silver bodies onto a rolling steel conveyor. They will not be wasted. They will become food. Note that. That makes it all OK.

The blood of the mothers needs to be washed off the eggs to prevent contamination.

None of this troubles Odd in the least. He's not even watching the film. He's pushing buttons on an interactive map and watching the rivers light up, red, orange, and green.

Once upon a time, the fish followed the smell of the river to the place they were born. That was once upon a time. Now they journey to the ocean and then they return to . . . To what? To a white plastic bucket? To a hatchery like this one? They return to spawn and to die, because that is what they do. They spawn and they die. That is what we all do. You can dress it up in a romance novel cover with moonlight shining on muscles and folds of flowing pink silk, but spawn and die, that's what we do. That is what we all do.

There are pools full of rainbow trout. A handful of fish-food pellets costs a quarter. Odd is amusing himself by making fish bump into each other. It's not hard; there are so many fish and the pool is so small. The rainbows hone in on the pellets and slither over each other in a rush. I take a picture of Odd beside the trout ponds. I could push a few buttons and send it to Buck. He'd have absolute proof that his little brother is safe and happy this very moment.

He could stop worrying, if he's worrying. I don't push any buttons. It might be the right thing to do, but Buck's happiness is not my problem. And Odd's happiness? It does belong to me, at least just a little bit.

A sign explains that the white spots on some of the fish are patches of fungal infection. The trout will be fine, says the sign. The water in the pond is medicated. All the water flows to the river, I guess, then to the ocean. When I look closely at the trout, I see fins that are ragged and rotten.

There is a little white house with a flight of stairs down into a room with big windows that look out underwater. It isn't an aquarium. It isn't a tank. There is a pond outside the windows that's deep and big enough for a ten-foot-long fish to roam around in. Herman the Sturgeon comes and goes, gliding past the windows and then away, into the green murk of the water.

He has company in there. There are other sturgeon, puny ones, not much bigger than me. Three big rainbows swim in place by one of the windows. There must be a current there that they keep pace with, swimming constantly, going nowhere. And there is another trout, a hunchback. The front end looks normal, but the tail end points down instead of straight back. It is able to swim. It has coping skills and strategies for its unusual condition.

Herman is the star, though. He is a monster. He meets the qualifications. Size? Check. Ugly? Check. He looks armor-plated, but he has a vulnerability—a monster always has a vulnerability. When he slides by on the other side of the glass, I can see into his gills where little red balloons full of blood cluster like horrible berries. There's a taped narration on infinite loop . . . Herman's kind shared the planet with dinosaurs in the Jurassic . . . they are threatened with global extinction . . . a single female can produce half a million eggs in a single season and it's not enough . . . they can't fight their way past the dams to spawning grounds.

A monster floats by on the other side of the window. He has a gummy, old-man mouth and four white, whiskery barbels to feel around for rotting food on the bottom of the pool. I lean my forehead on the cold glass and another monster floats reflected in the window. It's me. I want to bang my bony head on the glass, but it would never break. And what if it did? I couldn't save what's on the other side. I don't have the strength of an angel. I can't lift a four-hundred-pound fish. I can't move the Bonneville Dam. Maybe I want the monster on the other side to save me.

Odd stood in line for ice cream, and now we are sitting on a curb by some roses. Bees are assaulting and fumbling the flowers.

A few years ago all the honeybees were dying. Nobody understood it and it was a crisis, because if the bees disappear then all kinds of human food will disappear, like the peaches in my ice cream. There will be no more peaches if there are no more bees. But I don't know what happened. Maybe the bees stopped dying. Maybe they are still dying and we are moving closer every moment to a world without peaches. That seems more likely, that the bees are still dying, but the TV news turned its eye to a new place. That's the job of the news, to be new. So maybe the bees are still dying by hundreds and thousands, but what is new is sea turtles smothered in burning-hot crude oil or polar bears drowning because there is no ice. It's always something. And dead bees aren't very photogenic.

"Hey, Polly, Earth to Polly. Report," says Odd.

"I'm just thinking about peaches," I say.

"Yep! Good ice cream," says Odd, and he holds the cone out like a wineglass. I touch mine against his. "To Meriwether Lewis," says Odd, "who slept here in this exact spot, according to the sign."

"Do you think it's true?" I ask.

Odd shrugs. "It's cool to think about. Bet it looked different then." There's an interstate highway on one side and a giant dam blocking the river on the other. Odd's right. Things may have changed.

"Thomas Jefferson liked ice cream," says Odd, like that makes a difference.

Honeybees may be buzzing toward extinction. Thomas Jefferson made ice cream. The story is different for each of us.

On the way out of the hatchery, we pass Smokey Bear. He is standing by a fountain, handing out stickers to little kids. One little girl doesn't want anything to do with him. She hides her face against her dad's leg, wraps her arms around and won't come unstuck. Finally, the dad gives up and starts walking toward the parking lot. Hanging on her dad's leg turns into a game, and she starts laughing.

When there is a gap in the kid-and-sticker action, I get close and ask, "Is someplace close where I can fish? Trout, I mean, with a fly rod, no boat."

"I wish I'd known the answer to that one before I jumped at this job," says Smokey Bear. "I've seen some little ones at the bottom of the falls—Multnomah—but it's not worth it."

I wonder if Smokey is a liar. Maybe he doesn't want to share. Why should he?

"What about a good hike, pretty, not too far, not so many people?" I ask.

"McCord Creek, Elowah," says Smokey. Then he says, "You know the question I get asked most often? 'Where's the water come from?' That's what people want to know," Smokey waves paw at the cliff on the far side of the interstate. "'Where's the water come from?'" growls Smokey. "This stupid suit itches . . ."

"Got milt?" No, that isn't right. "Got *milk*?" says the winking cow on the back of the shiny tanker truck. No wonder she is so goddamn happy. She isn't a salmon. They don't kill her to steal what she's got. They just take her baby and the food she had to give it. She doesn't miss her calf. She would only miss her calf if her teats swelled up and hurt. They take care of that. They take the milk and haul it away and pasteurize it, which has nothing to do with a pasture full of grass. The cow is a machine to make milk. She doesn't need dirt or grass or sunshine to make milk. But people need milk to make ice cream.

ITSY-BITSY SPIDER:
McCord Creek

This is an easy trail—or it would be for Polly-That-Was and that kid Odd-With-Two-Legs, but they aren't here. It's a challenge for couch muscles, and couch muscles is what I've got. I can do it, but if I didn't have a real good reason, like a waterfall, I wouldn't go another step. I like green. I like ferns. I like the rotten cinnamon smell of the wet tree bark. But I've already got that. I had that at the edge of the parking lot.

I can hear kids' voices behind us. It's a happy family unit of parents, a little girl with cloth butterfly-fairy wings, and an even tinier person who will probably get lifted up and into a back carrier pretty soon. This is the kind of trail a toddler can own, and it's killing me.

While the family passes us by I'm careful to keep the bad side of my face turned away. I let Odd do the smiling and nodding and howdy. I can hide behind him and let him make eye contact to prove we are good people, decent people, just like them.

The decent family is on the way back down the trail. They've been to the waterfall—or given up and turned back early.

"The waterfall's great!" says the decent dad.

"Totally worth it," says the decent mom.

"Piedoo!" says the butterfly-fairy, pointing at the dirt.

"Yes!" says the decent dad, "A spider! That's great! He lives here in the woods. This is his home." He hunkers down by his butterfly-fairy child to look at the wonderful spider that lives in the woods.

Behind me, I can hear them singing, "Itsy-bitsy spider went up the water spout, down came the rain, and washed the spider out . . ."

If I couldn't see the creek and hear the waterfall, this is where I would stop.

We are close to an ancient volcano, the black rock here is pure, hexagonal pillars bending under the weight of miles of sky, and, where the black rock breaks, the water falls and bursts into spray. When the spray touches me, I'm not tired anymore. The mist collects on me into droplets and diamonds.

The waterfall is totally worth it. I leave the trail and pick my way closer to the bottom of the cliff. I can feel the force of the water moving through the rocks and up my legs. It is like breathing thunder.

Then I hear Odd, a barking yell. He should have stayed on the trail, but he didn't. He's on his hands and knees in the water and the rocks. His lips are flat and tight. His whole lower face has gone dead white. I've seen that before. I've seen that at the Kid-O-Korral when some bitch mom dropped her little guy off for Mom's Night Out and I discovered his arm was bruised, broken, when I took off his coat. I've seen it on my dad's face when he couldn't fix a horse that had been chained to a bumper and dragged for miles on asphalt. That is the face of a guy who is not going to cry even though there is damn good reason to do it.

"Come on." I get my feet planted securely and offer him a hand up. For a second he isn't going to take it. But then the fight goes out of him, his shoulders sag, he reaches out. It's not easy getting him over the slick black jags of rock. They are everywhere, like the teeth under a trout's tongue.

When we get to the trail, the battle should be over. The trail is wide and flat, not all that slippery most places.

"Can you put weight on it?"

He can't. It buckles and rolls out from under him. He says, "It's weird. It hurts. I can feel it, but it's like it's not there."

"Let me take a look at it." I prop him up, and we take a few awkward steps closer to the wooden bridge over the stream. Odd leans and steadies himself against the handrail.

It's hard to see through the rip in his jeans. He's definitely cut somewhere, although exactly where or how bad is a mystery kept by mud and blood and wet shadows. It probably looks worse than it is. That's what I tell the little kids when they scrape a knee or an elbow . . . looks worse than it is . . . really . . . it's going to be all healed up by to-morrow morning . . . your own body's going to make it better . . . how cool is that?

But this isn't the Kid-O-Korral. I don't have Band-Aids spotted with dinosaurs and puppies, even though choosing is part of the ritual that makes it all better. And I can't say the magic words, either. *Your own body's going to make it better.* I can't say that because the two of us, we know that's not always true.

Trails usually seem shorter when you are coming out than when you are hiking in. It doesn't matter if it's uphill or downhill, the time just moves faster. Usually that's true, but it isn't going to be like that this time. The trail to the parking lot gets longer with every awkward step. We aren't talking. I don't have the breath for it. Odd needs to keep his jaw clamped tight on the pain.

We are making progress. I'm counting the steps and pausing every hundred, sometimes less. If there is a good tree that Odd can lean against, that's a reason to stop. If we make it to the top of a slope, that's a reason to stop. If I feel Odd's muscles jerk to try to get away from the pain, that's a reason to stop, but I have to ignore that because we need to move sometime.

I could never walk side by side with Bridger. We were always out of sync. I always felt off balance, like I couldn't find my center of gravity. Other couples could do it. Other couples were well-oiled machines that could move together through the crowded halls between classes and then divide with a kiss. Other couples could float along together through the lights and music at the carnival like they were riding in the same bucket on a Ferris wheel. Or maybe that whole couple thing just looks simpler from the outside. Maybe those other girls were getting pulled around, too. Maybe it's never easy to have someone steer you around with a thumb through a belt loop and their fingers in your pocket. Maybe I'm making Odd's difficulties worse because I'm setting the pace and I'm the one with a death grip on his belt. Maybe, but if I don't do it, he isn't going anywhere. And if he isn't going anywhere, then his story stops moving down the trail. And I think then, when that happens, he's good as dead.

It's raining. Odd is shivering. I am not. Not yet. But I'm getting damn tired. This worse than steering a drunk. If Odd were drunk I'd worry less about him falling down. He is growing heavier and heavier. He's too much for me to carry, but that won't matter if I have to do it. We are both drenched by the time we hit the last little switchback in the trail.

The other cars are gone from the parking lot, but D'Elegance is waiting for us.

"Can you stand?" I ask. I don't get any real answer, but when I move his arm from my shoulder to the hood of the car, Odd props himself up. I don't know how long that's going to last. I steady him while I reach into his pocket for the keys. The wet denim of his jeans, the angle of my reach, my fingers have to fight their way into his right front pocket. There's nothing in there but a gaping hole at the bottom. I imagine the keys . . . squished into the mud on the trail someplace . . . shiny and invisible as water in the creek . . . in the other pocket . . . please, please. My fingers are cold and stiff, but the keys are there. I fish them out, hooked on my little finger.

The door to the plush interior of the car is wide open. I want to just push Odd in that direction and be done. My body is really ready to be done. I'm starting to feel the cold myself. The sound of drumming rain drowns out the sound of traffic on the interstate. The rain soaking my head is stealing the heat from my body. If we stay wet, the energy is going to bleed out of us. I'd feel dumb as hell if I let myself die of hypothermia in a parking lot.

"C'mon, Odd. Let's get you warm. OK?" I pull his wet T-shirt off him. He's gone all pale and blue and shaky. Then I unbutton his fly and start fighting the wet jeans down his legs. When I get them down around his ankles, I look up, right into the most vulnerable thing on the planet. Poor, pale, wet worm. Poor Odd. "Sit down in the car now, Odd. I need to get your boots and socks off. Here, let me look at that knee."

The cut isn't wide, but it might be deep. It's right under his kneecap. One of those sharp black points of rock got pushed up under there when he fell. Someplace else it might have just left a bruise, but in that place it caught somehow and broke the meat open. The nerves there, the tendons, who knows? Red-stained rain is following gravity in little rivers all the way to his ankle.

I've seen what I can see. I untie his boot and pull it off. I fumble around until his stump is free from his robot leg. I take off the robot leg so his stump won't be left sitting in the cold, wet socket. I nudge Odd's legs around until he's completely in the car. I shut the door. Then I just want a minute, but I can't have it.

Daylight doesn't last forever, not even in the summer, and it's starting to bleed away. With every minute the air is getting murkier and the world is getting flatter as the shadows dissolve. I wouldn't be surprised to see Herman the Sturgeon glide by outside the car in the remaining green light. It's that wet.

I open the trunk and grab the sleeping bags. Then I climb in and get Odd as covered up as I can. Odd does nothing to help.

We've got two choices: stay here in the Elowah parking lot or get back on the interstate and head to a place with food—maybe even a twenty-four-hour clinic if Odd doesn't perk up. How, exactly, is sitting in the parking lot doing nothing going to make things better? It's mostly open road, I figure, so I jack the seat into place and turn the key.

All I have to do is get to the on ramp and merge. I can merge. I can see what's coming. They'll have the lights on. And I can wait as long as I need to—I can wait until there are no lights. Then I just stay in the right lane until I get to a place that has what Odd needs, whatever that turns out to be. There isn't much traffic. It isn't super busy. But shit, the semis. They blow by me so hard the wake nearly pushes me off the road.

The rain comes down harder. The crappy blades can't push it off the windshield fast enough. The car wants to hydroplane. The tires are probably bald. Everything is original except the oil and gas. Thank you very much Gramma Dot, you sentimental lamebrain. If we die here, it's your fault, Gramma Dot—and you won't ever know. Or if you do know, you'll forget it, Gramma Dot, lucky you.

Troutdale is the first place that looks like it will work. Or at least the first place with more than one exit so I don't miss it by the time I should have turned.

Welcome to Troutdale, where all I have to do is drive around until I come to a place that sells Neosporin or

Betadine and Tylenol—and maybe cough syrup if I can get the kind that puts me to sleep. And there's a fast-food place open in the same mall. And parking isn't a problem because I pull into the wide-open spaces in the back forty, where nobody in their right mind would park on a rainy night. Lines shmines. Straight schmaigt. I kind of coast forward until I bump up onto the concrete median and it's good enough.

I turn to Odd. He looks pale in the watery light coming through the windshield. "You OK?"

"Not great."

"I'm going to get some stuff. You want to get dressed and come with—or you want to wait here?"

"I'll wait."

"I'll be back fast. You want me to leave the heater on? The radio?"

He doesn't answer, so I guess not. I leave the keys if he changes his mind.

"Look. Drink some of this. It's decaf. They didn't have tea, but I put a lot of milk in it so it should be cool enough to drink right now. And take these," I shake out two night-time pain tablets into my hand. He doesn't reach for them, but when I put my hand by his mouth he opens up and I tip them in. He lifts the coffee up and drinks by himself, though.

"I got you a burger and an apple pie if you want to eat."

"Maybe later."

"You want me to look at that cut? Make sure it's clean and dry? I got some stuff to prevent infection."

"Maybe later. The cut doesn't hurt. But my robot leg is on fire."

His robot leg isn't even connected.

"Those pills were for pain," I say. "They'll help."

"Not like the good stuff they used to put in the IV. That shit worked fine. Is there any whiskey left?"

"I don't think so."

"Could you check in the trunk? It could take the edge off."

"No. I won't. You can't mix Tylenol and alcohol. It will ruin your liver. Tylenol is dangerous that way. If you take too much it will kill you. Just because you can buy it everywhere doesn't make it safe."

"Really?" Odd picks up the Tylenol bottle from the dash and looks at it like it's suddenly more important. I take it away from him.

"This is the P.M. kind. You'll fall asleep pretty soon. The pain stops when you sleep, doesn't it? Give it a half hour."

"I could smoke a bowl."

"Yeah. I guess. If you want."

"I do. But it's in the trunk."

"That's OK. I'm already wet."

When I'm at the trunk I look at the Tylenol bottle in my hand. I shake out a couple for myself. They taste good, like vanilla tea. Then I dump the rest into the water that's streaming through the parking lot. It will go down the drain and into the river, like all the birth control and antidepressants and antibiotics. It will be in the water and nothing good will come of it. But there's no chance Odd will poison himself with it, either.

I find the ziplock with his pipe and prescription bottle in the Lucky Charms box. Whatever else he can do with this bud, he can't kill himself directly. Maybe he's right. Maybe it is good medicine. But I'm so wet, cold, and tired I don't have enough sense to get out of the rain. I should not operate a vehicle. I should not be practicing medicine without a license.

Odd is asleep. I will be soon. The rain is drumming on the car. The windows are fogging up. When we breathe, Odd and I, we breathe out water. The car is an aquarium at the bottom of the river. We are aquarium trout. Our fins are dissolving. Sad white lumps are growing over our mouths, over our eyes.

A shape moves by in the water outside of the windshield. Then it comes closer. The sturgeon's barbels move like gentle fingers over the wet glass in a blessing. The glass is no barrier, it dissolves, pulled apart by water and gravity. I can feel the barbels on my cheek, caressing my scar.

"You are beautiful, Polly." It's Odd, his hand on my face. He's half asleep. Probably delirious.

"Rest now, Odd. We both need to sleep."

"Could you sing, Polly?"

"I'll turn on the radio . . ."

"No, Polly, just go ahead and sing. I just need to hear your voice."

So I sing . . .

"Come away, human child
To the water and the wild
With a faery, hand in hand,
For the world's more full of weeping
  than you can understand."

I stop. Odd doesn't say anything. I listen to the rain and wait for sleep to come again. I wait, and I think about sturgeon. Their plan worked for millions of years, so they kept moving up the current into the future. Then the dams came and the future wasn't where it used to be. The old plan doesn't work anymore. I think about MRSA, too, the latest generation of something older than sturgeon. When the world changes, MRSA changes. It adapts. Try to kill it, and it reinvents itself. I wonder if maybe there is a sturgeon somewhere that is thrashing up a new channel to a new future. I wonder if, maybe, I can do that too.

DROP SHOT SINKERS:
Morrison Bridge

"You OK? I got you some more coffee. High octane this time."

Odd pulls his sleeping bag down from where it covered his face. "Yeah," he says. "I'm alright."

"How's the knee?"

"Hurts a little. Stiff. But it feels like I own it," he says and sits up to reach for the coffee. He looks good for somebody I thought was going to die.

"Do you have the address?"

"What address?"

"The address where that douche Bridger works. You know, the place we are going?"

"No," I say, but I don't say the rest of it, which that I'm not going to see Bridger. There is no point in trying to reach him. Bridger isn't my future. My river doesn't run in his direction. I'm over him. He is a douche. That's for certain, but it doesn't matter. He isn't my problem. He can find someone else and become her problem. He probably already has. It doesn't matter. I'm over it. I'm over him. I don't need revenge. I don't need to appear all scarred and stained with blood and chocolate pudding to yell at Bridger because he doesn't love me. But Odd doesn't know that. He's still pretty excited about the whole thing going down. As far as he knows, that's still The Plan.

I need to stall.

"I'm hungry. Let's eat."

"Yeah," says Odd, "and we can figure out where we are going, too. We need a plan. There's a place here somewhere that sells bacon doughnuts."

"Well, get your pants on then. I'd just as soon you do the driving if you can," I say.

"Me too," says Odd.

Traffic is streaming around us and we are streaming with it. Should we take this exit? The next one? Is there going to be a sign marked "Bacon Doughnuts"?

"I think I need something more like food than a doughnut," I say.

"Thai?" Odd points down the cross street.

"That's a one-way."

"Crap, how do we get back on the interstate?"

"Just follow the arrows."

"Morrison Bridge, that looks good, we'll take that."

But first we're stuck at a stoplight beside a real estate business. The sign says, "Home is only the beginning." The light changes and Odd heads out. We act like we have a plan. And we do, at the moment. Pretty soon we are crossing the Willamette. If I were a fish, I would know I was heading the wrong direction. The waters of the Willamette would not smell right. They would not smell like home.

It isn't easy to park D'Elegance on the street. She's a pre-historic pig. She wants more room than a delivery van. Once we find a space big enough, we still need to figure out how the parking meter ticket thingy works.

"No biggy," says Odd. "It doesn't matter.

"It's the law," I say

"Seriously? You know the license plates on the car expired ten years ago, right? Look, we'll eat right over there." He points at a pizza place. "If somebody comes around to write a ticket, we'll just explain. We'll explain how you don't like to break the law. I'm sure they will be real impressed."

Some things never change. Odd might be one of them.

"I need to find an ATM. We'll probably need cash for the pizza. You can wait for me there."

And he does. When I get back I find him in front of a pinball machine. *The Sopranos* it says. How much story is there in a pinball game? Does having pictures of fat old gangsters on it make it more fun? It isn't like there is some sad chick with big hair crawling away on her knees in the woods and when it goes TILT she gets shot in the head. Or is it?

The pizza is hot. Big leaves of fresh basil are wilting in the steam rising up from the tomato sauce and cheese.

"I'm done," I say.

"What you mean?" asks Odd. "You didn't even eat any of it yet. Then he picks up a piece of pizza bigger than his head, folds it, and steers the point into his gullet.

"No, Odd. Not the pizza," I pick up a piece of my own. The food smells good, full of heat and life. The cheese stretches out like a suspension bridge from the slice in my hand to the pieces waiting in the pan. I break the connection. "I'm just totally done. I'm going home."

I hand him a wad of bills. It's as much as I could get out of the ATM, minus the cost of pizza. I hand it to him while I get my stuff out of the car and shove it into a big black trash bag that was in the trunk. There are some coffee cups and chip bags in the bag already. I don't care.

Odd doesn't say anything. He just stands there with his hand full of twenties. Maybe he thinks I just want him to hold it while I get myself organized.

I touch his hand so he understands. "You can spend it on a tattoo. You can spend it on bacon doughnuts. But there's enough there to get gas if you want to go home," I say.

He shoves it in his pocket. "You ever seen the ocean, Polly? Because we are that close. It's crazy to come this far and not see the ocean."

"I've seen the ocean," I say.

"We could go all the way like Lewis and Clark. We could go to Cape Disappointment. You seen Cape Disappointment?"

Cape Disappointment? That question is harder to answer than it ought to be. I saw the ocean from a sand dune beside Monterey Bay. My dad was holding my hand, and he said there were seals and otters and sharks out there, even whales. We were going to the aquarium to see them. But the sharks were only babies and there weren't any whales, except for bones. So I've been to Cape Disappointment lots of times, I think. Who hasn't? I look at Odd's face and try to read out why he wants to go there. There is something pure about his face, pure like a river ought to be. There is nothing hiding there, I think. He just wants to see something that hasn't changed since Lewis and Clark saw it. And the ocean hasn't changed because it never holds still. There is no good reason why Odd shouldn't do what he wants.

"If you go to Cape Disappointment, you might not have enough money to make it all the way home. But that's OK. You just get as close as you can and then you call me. Like, if you get as far as Missoula and you can't get back, you call me. I'll come get you."

"Hey." The hug surprises me. It feels for real. It feels good, and before I move away I rest my forehead under his collarbone on his chest. I can hear his heart inside my head, but it is probably my imagination.

"Hey," I say. And then I pick up my garbage bag and my rod case. It is time to go.

"Hey," says Odd, "Can you do me a solid? Can you give these letters to my Gramma Dot? I don't know what her address is going to be when she gets back. You know? So if you could take them, you could get them to her, since you're going that direction."

"Yeah, I can do that," I say. I wait while he pulls the pages out of a little notebook he carries in his pocket. He folds them up into a crooked wad and holds them out to me.

Then I pick up my garbage bag and my rod case. It's time for me to go.

On the streets of Portland there is really nothing weird at all about a grubby girl carrying her stuff in a black plastic garbage bag. Here I could pass for normal, almost, until someone got a good look at me. But really, nobody looks that hard at a grubby girl and her garbage bag—at least not on this street at this time of day.

But I'd like to pass for normal in the airport. A normal person does not board a plane carrying a rod case and a garbage bag. A garbage bag is not a conventional carry-on.

Luggage. It is my lucky day, the sign across the street says, "Luggage."

I get pretty immediate attention, as a grubby girl should in a not-so-grubby place. "Give me the cheapest duffle this big." I hold my hands out like I'm telling a fish story, a fish story big enough to hold my sleeping bag , fishing vest, and tent.

He looks a little suspiciously at my debit card—and then at my face. I lay the driver's license of Polly-That-Was on the counter. Then I put my Montana fishing license beside it. The signatures match.

The transaction is complete.

"Where can I catch transport to the airport?"

The guy points.

"Thanks. Got it."

But I have one more thing to do.

I stop at the green park by the river's edge and dump out my stuff. I fold the garbage bag and put it on the ground beside the trash can. I weigh it down with a rock so it won't blow away. It's a resource. Someone might be able to use it. Then I rummage in the foot of my sleeping bag. The gun is in one bloody sock and the ammo in the other. I take them out and put them on my lap, and then I zip the duffle shut.

When I stand up, I'm a grubby girl with a duffle slung on my shoulder, my rod case in one hand, and a pair of lumpy, dirty socks in the other. I could just drop the socks and their burden in the trash can beside me, but I don't want anyone to find the gun and maybe use it. It's a resource that shouldn't be loose in the world. I owe that much to the other grubby girls and wandering boys.

There isn't that much foot traffic on the Morrison Bridge. I sort of hate being here. I know it's just because I can't see very well, but the gust of force and exhaust when the trucks pass feels strong enough to knock me off my feet. I just promise myself that I will get far enough to be over deep water, deep enough water.

The air below me is deep—my body knows it even if my eye can't see it. The further I go, the deeper the air, the deeper the water. This is deep enough. I crowd the rail, stand on my toes, and lean to look over the edge. I feel the tug of gravity and the dizzy spinning that comes from not trusting what I see. And something else: just for a moment I let myself feel how much I desire falling, how much I feel the impulse to—just let myself go. There's a future down there, and it would be so easy to be finished with it. The little voice inside my head is whispering, "Yes. Yes." And I'm listening. I admit it. I've been carrying that hitchhiker the whole time. I pretended it was Odd, by all logic it should have been Odd, but it was inside of me, that little suicidal whisper.

I grab that impulse. I hook my fingers deep in its gills, and I'm the one in control. I'm the one who gets to decide if I live or die.

I get to decide.

There isn't a boat directly below me. I drop the socks. I'm so high up, and the light on the water is so flat, I can't even see a splash. I hope nobody else saw it either. The damn gun is gone, and Odd was alive the last time I saw him, and that's the whole story. At least the part of it I know.

The souvenir T-shirt is pink as a marshmallow heart and says, "Girls Fish Too!" My mom always said I looked pretty in pink, because *all* redheads look pretty in pink. I always thought it made me look like a strawberry milkshake. The shirt's pink, but it's on sale. That makes it perfect. It matches my scar. Pink is my new favorite color. I buy a hairbrush, too. And a tiny bottle of mouthwash.

I strip off my dirty shirt and shove it in the trash in the airport bathroom. I swish the mouthwash around. I wash my face and arms. Then I try to brush my hair, what's left of it.

There are yards of mirrors over the sinks in the bathrooms. There are big full-length mirrors on the exit wall. I look at myself. I've looked worse. It won't matter much anyway, since most people won't even see me. I'm just another invisible stranger. I can walk through the airport. I can go anywhere. I can go to Ireland to look for talking trout or to Siberia to see sturgeon. Home is only the beginning. That's where it starts. So I'm going there and I'm going to start. So I pick up my rod case and go to the gate for my flight.

I'm waiting in an airport. Just like all the people around me. I'm waiting, and I have nothing to read—except the wad of letters to Gramma Dot.

Boulder River

Dear Gramma Dot,

Wish you were here. I bet you wish you were here too, because here is a good place to be. It's a blue-sky day. I'm on the Boulder down by the Natural Bridge. That girl Polly and me came up here to do some fishing. Seems like they ought to be biting, but they aren't buying what I'm selling. Maybe it's a little too hot or they're all full to the gills with grasshoppers because I got nothing.

I drove G-pa Odd's car up here—I figure you don't mind—you said it was going to be mine when I needed it. That car is like driving a big old chunk of heaven, like you already know.

Stopped to see the prairie dog show on the way over. Polly didn't seem too impressed. She thinks she's going to get the plague off them. Normal person would see cute. That Polly, she sees a tick bus full of disease. Anyhow, Hokahey! like Crazy Horse said. It's a good day.

So you remember when you brought me here the first time? I do. I remember you told me that there used to be a real natural bridge made of rock that went from one side of the river to the other. You told me about how there was a fieldtrip and a bus full of kids went over to the other side to have a picnic. After the picnic, when they were all in the bus, the bridge fell down and just crashed down into the river. If it happened ten minutes earlier all them kids would have died, but they didn't.

We found some real good fossils in the riverbed that day. I still got mine. Then we climbed up to that cave and saw those paintings, the red ones. And you said they couldn't be too ancient because one of them showed a gun, but they were still cool. The cave was cool too, the air in it I mean. And you told me that was what bat shit smells like and not to stir up the dust. I still remember all about that day. It was a good day too. A real good day.

And today is a real good day. I saw some prairie dogs, and I hiked down here to this hole below the falls, and since the fish aren't cooperating I'm sitting on this rock by the river and writing to you.

Love, your boy Odd

Firehole River

Dear Gramma Dot,

Started out the day with some biscuits and gravy, but they weren't nearly good as you make. Not even after I put on a lot more pepper. They don't know your secret ingredients.

The reason I'm writing today is that you might hear from some people how I'm not acting responsible. That's one way to look at it, I guess, but I got another, and the way I look at it is Buck doesn't need my help and I sure don't need his. I was going down to the dealership just like I was supposed to, but all Buck ever had me do was vacuum the sales office and make coffee—and they got a janitor service and Diane in the office makes better coffee than me—or so I got told. So mostly I was just standing around doing nothing. That gave me plenty of time to hear Buck saying about how I used to have a future but that's over now. He'd say it right in front of me like I was rig with a busted axle and trading up was a better idea because what's the point of fixing it. I just got a little tired of that. I don't care if it was helping him make sales or not. He used to get people to buy equipment before I was available to look pathetic so he can just go back to doing whatever works.

So anyhow I need to figure out what works for me. What works today is some more fishing.

Me and that girl Polly came down the Paradise through the park to the Firehole. Stopped at Mammoth Hot Springs on the way in and the minerals were all sparkly in the sunshine. It occurred to me that maybe this was the mountains of salt that Lewis and Clark thought they'd find, so I mentioned that to some tourists, but the whole story was news to them. I also told them about how Lewis and Clark thought they would be finding wooly mammoths. The world was a pretty big place back then and nobody knew what was in it.

I kept an eye out for mammoths, but all I saw was a badger and a buttload of slow-moving buffalo. Spent time out on the river, but I still didn't catch anything. I got distracted by some pretty girls from Japan who were taking pictures. Polly didn't catch anything either, but I don't know what distracted her. She doesn't talk much. She isn't shy—more pissed off and stuck up.

Basically, it was a good day—a whole lot better than it would have been making coffee at the dealership.

Love, your boy Odd

Out by Elkhorn

Dear Gramma Dot,

It's getting light, but it still ain't warm so I'm not going to get up for a while. It's OK here in the sleeping bag, and I don't mind burning daylight. Got a headache or I'd go back to sleep. Took some aspirin and a drink of water and that should kick in a while, but right now, I remembered you saying that doing something keeps the mind off the pain. So what I'm doing is writing to you.

One reason I might have a headache is because that girl Polly flew off the handle and whacked me in the head. She goes from mopey to dangerous faster than a snake. I never saw that coming, tell you what. She's sad and she's mad—I get that. But the worst thing is she doesn't appreciate anything. On top of that she's got a stick up her butt like you wouldn't believe.

Like yesterday we went to Elkhorn, which you know is a cool place because you showed it to me. Some things have changed. I looked all around in the cemetery, and I didn't see a jar full of lemons and vinegar on any of the graves. Not even any broken glass. I remember what you said about how we can't know if there is a heaven or a hell, but if there is a hell there are way more people who deserve to be in it. I remember what you said about that grave and how the vinegar and lemons was left on it by people he'd hurt.

They left that there as a way to remember but also get rid of the memories. I thought about that and then I peed on the grave I think was the right one. I figure it's the thought that counts.

Polly didn't like that.

Did a little target practice. Polly didn't like that either.

Then while she was supposed to be getting a fire together so we could make some dinner, she kicked me in the head with my own foot and gave me a bloody nose.

She's a handful of crazy. But I remember you told me crazy isn't the same as bad and most crazy comes from being afraid. So I gave her the gun and told her nobody could make her do what she didn't want to do. We'll see how that turns out.

Love, your boy Odd

Blackfoot River

Dear Gramma Dot,

I remember you told me that dreams are just my brain flushing the toilet and that I should just wake up and forget them, but sometimes that's not so easy to do. Last night I dreamed I was little again and Buck was going shove my head in the toilet like he tried to do that one time when he bashed my face on the rim so hard I nearly bit my own lip off.

But then—because it was a dream, and dreams don't make sense, like you always said—the toilet turned into a cat box and Buck made me eat a cat turd. Then after that I had to do whatever Buck told me until he fell asleep. But I couldn't run away because I couldn't find my robot leg. I don't know what I needed it for because in the dream I had my own two legs, but I woke up needing to find it. I still had it on. That just proves you are right about dreams. But that dream did remind me about something I need to tell you, but I been avoiding it.

It's about your kitty, Cat Ballou.

Buck told me I was supposed to take Cat to the vet and get her put down. He said it needed done because you can't take her with you to the new place, and nobody wants to deal with her because she's so old and smells bad. I said I'd take care of her, but he said "no way" and I'm not responsible and besides she just dribbles pee. He said Dad left money for the vet and if I didn't take her, he'd keep the money and throw her in a dumpster. Wouldn't even cost a bullet, he said. But it was supposed to be my job to deal with it.

So I took her. But I took her to a place called a no-kill shelter. When I explained, they seemed real nice and said they knew how to care for old kitties like her. They asked me though, if I could take a dog so there would be room. That particular dog is a little too much high energy to be living with cats. So I said, sure, why not? It wasn't until I got that dog home that I remembered what Buck did to the last one. So I just traded one problem for another. It's OK though, because then I traded that dog for Polly. Like I said, I just traded one problem for another one.

They say you can visit Cat Ballou there at the shelter. Like I said. They seemed real nice.

I have a bear of a headache, and as soon as Polly gets back I'm gonna get me a cup of coffee somewhere down the road.

Mostly yesterday was a real good day. Hokahey! I'm gonna see what today is good for as soon as I get that coffee.

Love, your boy Odd

St. Regis River

Dear Gramma Dot,

That Polly is the only person I know who gets more cranky after she pees. I went into a flyshop to find out what the fish were biting on and when I came back she about bit my head right off. I got no positive idea why. But I got to step up and own some responsibility. I did mention as how her dad might have had a hand brewing up the MRSA. It's true and all that, but I could have maybe not said it and avoided some trouble. Polly didn't want to hear about it. She gave me a look that'd peel the paint off a cue ball. It was all downhill from there, and she's on a tear again.

I'm pissed off my own self, for my own reasons.

Buck's figured out I'm with Polly.

And then my cup of coffee sucked. I think maybe the water they made it with is bad because the Clarksfork around there used to be full of toxics that came all the way from Butte. That's a bad deal, poison running through rivers just like an infection in the blood. Then they take that water and sell it for coffee.

My head still hurts. I just chewed up four aspirin and washed them down with water right out of the river. I don't know if there's any fish in there, but that water is cold enough to freeze my teeth and give me a headache if I didn't already got one.

So I wish you was here. I don't know if you ever saw this place, and you might like it. More important, I think you'd tell me to pull my head out of my ass. Somehow, just me pretending that you said to do it doesn't do the trick.

Love, your boy Odd

Spokane, Washington (kind of near Thor Street)

Dear Gramma Dot,

   Right now I'm in Spokane. I remember us being
here before and going to a big park where there was
a little kangaroo in a petting zoo pen. It was a hot day
and that kangaroo didn't do a single thing but flop
in the shade and pant. It's kind of a raw deal being a
kangaroo in Spokane. The rest of the kangaroos are on
the other side of the planet. I never thought about that
when I was a kid and we were here together.

   That was the day you put me on an amusement
ride and then worried the whole time I was on it that I
was going to slide right out because I was skinny as a
snake. The funny thing is, I don't have my own memory
about being on that ride. When I think about it, it's like
I'm seeing me from the outside and any minute I'm
going to end up hanging on for dear life and flapping
like a rag while the ride spins around and I'll just be
there watching it happen.

   Polly snores, it turns out. I bet she won't believe it
if I tell her in the morning, but she snorks like a critter
with no shame.

   Her latest deal is she cut her hair off and threw it
out the window while we were driving down the road.

   I don't know what that was all about.

   I remember you taught me sometimes we got
to take care of somebody despite what they do, not

because of it. The snoring and the random hair cutting and pure ornery is all part of the deal.

Love, your boy Odd

The intersection of Wheat and more Wheat, Washington

Dear Gramma Dot,

I'm just going to take a minute to tell you that I was bit by a snake today. It's not so bad as it was in the old days on the Oregon Trail. It bit me in the robot leg, and so I'm unlikely to die. I still didn't like it. It'd be fine with me if I never get snakebite again.

And I was thinking about Thea and wondering if she might still be in Reno and if there is any way to find her. Probably not, because if she wanted to be found, she'd make it easier to do it.

We can make Portland tomorrow. I might know what I'm going to do next by then, but I sure don't know now. It's not a bad thing. I'm OK with not knowing.

Polly saw a shooting star.

I'm going to settle down and sleep right here in G-Pa Odd's car. That way you don't need to worry about me having another run-in with a snake. You don't need to worry.

Love, your boy Odd

I fold the pages into an Odd-style wad. He said not to worry. He said that because he loves her; he loves Gramma Dot. She loves him, and he knows she might worry. Love is all tangled up with worry, but you can't cast out into the world until the line is untangled. I take my phone out and set to work. "Mom? You're going to love my new pink shirt."

Even though there are other empty seats by the gate, a guy comes and sits beside me and nudges me a little. I turn to him. He points at my rod case. That's where he's looking. Everything else about me is irrelevant.

"Been fishing?" he asks.

"Yup."

"Trout?"

"Yup."

"Any big ones?"

"Troutzilla," I say, "I caught Troutzilla. Catch and release."

Acknowledgments

Thank you, Andrew Karre. You are an excellent guide; when I cast where you point, something always rises.

Thank you to all the book-building geniuses at Carolrhoda Lab—Julie, Danielle, Lindsay, and Elizabeth. It was real luck to land with you.

Thank you, Smokey Bear. I remember fondly the time when you compared me to a wheezing schnauzer panting after scientific proof. We are perfect for each other.

Thank you, Bill The Muse. You are so brilliant I have to punch you sometimes.

Thanks and apologies to the fishing poets, living and dead.

Finally, thank you, my little trout in the pool at Twin Creeks. I know you ate the Cheerios I threw to you only because you were generous. I hope you got big as Herman the Sturgeon. I know you are out there, Troutzilla.

About the Author

Blythe Woolston works as a professional book indexer for academic presses. She is the author of *The Freak Observer*, which won the ABC New Voices Pick award, the Moonbeam Children's Book Award, and the 2011 William C. Morris YA Debut Award. She lives in Montana with her family. Visit her online at www.blythewoolston.com.

ES JUN 04 2012

JAN 1 6 2013 YO

KL APR 1 5 2013